MW00939326

AN UNEXPECTED BRIDE

"Her debut novel, An Unexpected Bride, has burst onto the scene, zooming up the bestseller lists and racking up fans faster than other writers racking up words....a smash hit!"
- KINDLE FIRE DEPARTMENT

"Author Shadonna Richards has an "unexpected" bestseller on her hands with this unheralded romantic comedy....An Unexpected Bride has sold 10,000 copies in its first three months..."
-KINDLE NATION DAILY

"Shadonna Richards is a wonderful author!...It's a sweet and romantic story that will sweep you off your feet."
- REVIEWS BY MOLLY

"This sweet and humorous romance is sure to keep you entertained as well as have you giggling"
– TWEEZLEREADS

"I would recommend this book to fans of chick-lit and light romance or anyone looking for a book to curl up with on a rainy afternoon."
-HANDS AND HOME

"If you love a romance that's filled with laughs, ups, downs, twists and turns then this is for you. I am now a fan of Shadonna Richards and I can't wait to see what she has in store for her readers next!"
-REVIEWS BY MOLLY

"...an endearing story about a devoted granddaughter wanting to give her grandfather his last wish... Pick up a copy and experience Shadonna's writing!"
--Barb (SUGARBEATS BOOKS)

"For me, this was one of those books you cuddle up with on a stormy day, with your favorite beverage in your favorite chair, and just get lost in the story…a fun read." **--TWEEZLEREADS**

"This is a well-written story that flows along nicely..."-**THE SCARF PRINCESS**

AN UNEXPECTED BRIDE

Shadonna Richards

Copyright © 2010 Shadonna Richards

All rights reserved; no part of this publication may be
reproduced or transmitted by any means, electronic, mechanical,
photocopying or otherwise, without the prior permission of the
publisher.

This book is a work of fiction. The names, characters, places,
and incidents are products of the writer's imagination or have
been used fictitiously. Any resemblance to persons, living or
dead is entirely coincidental.

ISBN: 1463774826
ISBN-13: 9781463774820

ACKNOWLEDGMENTS

Thank you, God for all my blessings. To my cherished son and husband for your unconditional love. With gratitude to my family and friends for your endless support. To Solomon, Jermaine, Merdella, Nesitta, Godwin, Monica, and Percell. To my editor Marielle Marne for always being brilliant.

SHADONNA RICHARDS

"...It is better to marry, than to burn with passion."
– 1 Corinthians 7:9 (NIV)

1

"You mean to tell me, you can't find a decent man? Not one?"

"Grampa!" Emma Wiggins felt the blood siphon from her face. She could not believe she was having this conversation.

She shifted her hips uncomfortably on the hospital bedside of her ailing grandfather, trying to find the right words to say. She knew quite well where he was going with his comment. He was desperate to see her settle down, get married and have kids one day. But after her previously tainted relationships left her with emotional burns to 70 percent of her heart, no way was she going down that yellow brick road to happiness again. There's no place like home...alone.

"Oh, Gramps!" she whispered, tilting her head to the side, gently stroking his wrinkled forehead with her free hand as if comforting a fragile kitten.

"Look, I promise you, I won't end up...dying alone and penniless. You have my word on it—okay?"

Her whispered reassurance was virtually inaudible as she ingested what seemed like a handful of sand in her throat. Was that a promise she could even keep? She wanted to give him hope, something to cheer about. Especially now as he neared the end of his long time battle with what he called "a dreadful opponent that had a habit of sneaking up at the wrong time—prostate cancer."

The long-term care unit at Mercy Springs Memorial Hospital was unusually quiet during the busy lunch hour. The place was tranquil except for the sound of the air conditioner gently humming in the background and the odd clanking of knives scraping plates as some patients ate their meals. The aroma of hospital food filled the air. The scent of fresh cut flowers she'd bought and placed at the bedside table wafted to her nostrils. She eyed his untouched lunch tray. The smell of mashed potato with gravy and sliced beef reminded her she hadn't eaten.

Laced with guilt, Emma glanced down at her watch. She didn't want to leave him. Not ever. Not after what the doctor told her about his prognosis. But she didn't want to push her luck at work either. Her boss, Evan Fletcher, president of Fletcher Advertising where she worked as an account executive had been more than kind already to extend her lunch hour to visit her ailing Gramps. They had the pivotal conference call meeting in half an hour with one of their biggest potential clients. She didn't want to blow this. Not now.

This was a career clincher for her. But speaking of careers.... Her grandfather, whom she'd always referred to as Gramps when she was a little girl and had trouble pronouncing Grandpa, just finished a fresh round of chastising his only granddaughter for putting career ahead of love and family. If only he knew. She would love to have a family and a husband. But…

Her grandfather, Mr. Wiggins, reclined weakly and peered at her with droopy eyelids. His favorite pair of thick brown spectacles propped on the tip of his nose. He felt comfortable with them on, even when resting. The head of his bed elevated to a ninety degree angle. The green and white hospital bed sheets covered him up to his chest. He hadn't eaten much during the past few days. He appeared older than his eighty years. Emma knew her grandfather loved her and wanted the best for her. She was also painfully aware that he regretted only having one child, a son, Emma's father. Oh, she looked like her dad. Deep, almond shaped brown eyes that sparkled, dark, curly long ebony hair that shined. And a dimpled smile to melt even the coldest of hearts. Always willing, always helpful.

"I know that silly guy hurt you when he left you but—"

"Oh, Gramps. Why are you talking about that now? I'm so over him." She emphasized the "so" and bit down on her lower lip. She wished she could simply delete the bitter memory of her ex-fiancé's betrayal from her mind. She longed to erase the baggage of emotional scars he packed her off with. Yes, her hope was singed during that nasty breakup period, but she couldn't dwell on relationships now. Her work was her love. And so was Gramps.

"Sometimes you need to take your messed up relationships with a grain of grace so you can appreciate when the right one comes along. I just don't want to see you let him ruin your chances of happiness with someone else. In hindsight, I can say that other guy was a goof, not worthy of you!" He struggled to lean forward and touched her cascading mane of dark, spiralling curls.

Emma was amazed at his strength. She didn't realise that many palliative patients had energy before their inevitable demise. In fact, she was always in amazement when she visited the quiet unit. Patients were up and about, walking, conversing, and partaking of typical activities. Of course, not all patients were responsive and ambulatory. It was a mixture of diagnosis, prognosis, and illness processes. The ages of the patients ranged from eighteen-years-old to those who reached their ninety-ninth year.

"You realise you're my only grandchild." A muffled cough emitted from his throat. He grabbed a tissue from the side table and covered his mouth with it, coughed up, and wiped his mouth clean before tossing the Kleenex in the black garbage bin by his bedside. "The Wiggins line will be finished if you don't marry and have kids, pumpkin," he emphasised tearfully, water filling his eyes. Emma could barely watch him cry.

Just then, one of the nurses, a perky redhead sporting bright pink scrubs, bought in a plate with a slice of cake on it. Her cheeks glowing red.

"Oh, what's the occasion?" Emma was glad to change the subject as she peered at the icing on the cake.

"Oh, this is from Mr. Harry next door. His granddaughter just got married in the room."

"Married? Here?"

"Yes." The nurse placed the cake on the table before the untouched tray of food. "We sometimes get requests for wedding ceremonies to take place at the bedside for palliative patients who are too ill to otherwise attend. He wanted to give his daughter away. We arranged for the chaplain to do the honors, but sometimes patient's family members bring in their own minister." The nurse smiled and fixed Emma's grandfather's pillow and repositioned him before darting out of the room.

Emma couldn't help but notice her grandfather's fresh round of tears.

"What's wrong, Gramps?" Surprise caught her voice.

"I just wished it were you, pumpkin. It's my only wish before I go to be with your dear old grandma to see you get married, settle down, have a family. You're hiding yourself in your work. There's so much more to life than work, you know. We all need love, pumpkin. It won't be nice to be alone when I'm gone—" His voice cracked and broke off. "I just hate to think you'll be alone with no one. Just don't give up too easy on finding true love."

Emma's heart took a serious plunge into the deep end of despair. She could bear no more. If only he knew it was just as unsettling to her as it was to him to see her in this state.

Lord knows she tried hard to make things work with her ex-fiancé, of whom she could barely bring herself to recite his name. But, oh, nothing escaped the careful observation of her grandfather. He knew her all too well.

Truth was, she really *did* hide behind her work, bury herself in its corporate arms, lose herself to the company's aims and objectives.

But it was the perfect cover. And why not? She'd at least be doing some good service while keeping her mind busy at the same time.

Why not pour her heart into working to change images through advertising? Fulfill a need. Utilize her communications skills to write and design advertisements for special clients to inform the public about products and services that could help them to make their lives better. Contribute to economic growth. Yes, there were some things much more critical than love, Emma tried to convince herself.

Still, she really couldn't live with herself knowing the doctor told her in the family meeting earlier that Gramps only had days to live. Days! How could she not want to see him happy?

Her large, tearful brown eyes surveyed his aging, graceful face as if each blessed, earned wrinkle had a story of its own to tell. Her eyes penetrated his dark, kind, tired eyes glazed over with cataracts. At one time, this same pair of eyes was so filled with life. Love. Hope.

He was all she had now.

She was all he had.

Those time-honoured crow's-feet in the corners of his eyes ever so present. Each representing wisdom and sacrifice made to his country. His family.

"Gramps, don't worry. I'm…I'm okay. I-"

His tears fell hard like the Texas rain. Her grandfather bellowed out in pain. Her grandfather, the stronghold of the family, loving, determined, but wore his heart on his shirt sleeves, was never afraid to weep. That took a powerful man to do that. This same man took her in when everyone else—meaning her parents—could not care for her.

Soon, the nurse would come back in and wonder what Emma did to upset this poor, dying man.

"Gramps, I didn't want to tell you before but…I'm seeing someone. I am getting married." *Liar.*

Emma bit down on her full, defined lips. Anything to make him happy—a dying man's last wish. But before Emma could stop herself, she swallowed another hard lump of reality. What did she just do? Did she just tell a lie to spare his feelings? She could shoot herself. But she hoped he didn't hear amongst his own wailing.

As if someone turned off a faucet, his flow of tears almost dried up immediately.

"What did you just say, darlin'?" He sniffled and grabbed a tissue at the bedside to dab at his tears, his shaky hand removed his spectacles while the other free one wiped his eyes.

"I'm…you know…" Hesitation. Crackles shadowed her vocal chords.

"Getting married? Sweetheart, that's wonderful news. Why didn't you tell your dear old Gramps before? Getting me all worried. Who's the lucky guy? What's his name?" He peered over his spectacles. A light seemed to beam from his face.

Okay, now what do I say?

"Um…"

Think, Emma. Think.

"Evan." She could kick herself. By the time she was through she would be beaten and worn.

"Evan who?"

Okaaay.

"Fletcher." *Good Lord. Okay, now I've done it. What's wrong with me?*

She tried to convince herself she wasn't entirely dishonest. She was seeing her sexy, heart-stopping, gorgeous boss Evan for the sole purpose of work—every day. They worked closely at the agency for the past three years—sometimes late nights to meet tight deadlines, travelling together. He'd promoted her from new grad receptionist to office manager to account coordinator and possibly more. He'd always believed in her. She admired him from afar. Though Evan was as distant as a star in the galaxy from Earth. Okay, so he was a self-professed bachelor who had made it known to staff he despises the institution called marriage. He'd never know about this little secret lie she just spilled out to her grandfather.

Emma's BlackBerry vibrated with a gentle hum. It was the office. Evan probably wanted to know where she was—since they had that important conference call shortly.

"I'd *love* to see him," her grandfather blurted out. "When are you going to bring him by so that we can meet?"

Emma's entire body stiffened.

2

Emma drove back to the office in a daze. *What did I just do? I told my grandfather I was getting married to the president of my company. Have I taken leave of my senses?*

She didn't know how she arrived at the reserved parking lot at the Hope Plaza in Mercy Springs, Texas where the Fletcher Advertising Corporation, or FAC, building situated itself. The warm April sun glazed her skin as the gentle spring breeze whisked her curls in her face and flapped her opened satin trench coat. Her hands were in the pockets while her bag swung over her shoulder. She flipped her hair back as she walked away from her car and whisked up the stairs to the fourth floor. She bypassed taking the elevators to the top floor of the four-story plush building. Ordinarily, she was cheery and cracked a joke with the doormen. Not now. Her mind was bursting at the seams with too much in her head.

Her grandfather.

Her client meeting.

Evan.

"Evan's in the conference room waiting for you," Lucinda, one of the two receptionists at the front desk informed her as she walked in through the double glass door.

"Right. Thanks, Lucinda." Emma regretted she didn't have time to use the ladies room to make sure her face was relaxed and her makeup still intact. She also hoped Lucinda, the wonderful office career receptionist, administrator and full-time office gossip didn't notice her dazed expression. She tried to keep a distance of a thousand words from the woman who staff members often referred to as "loose-lips-Lucinda."

Got a secret? Lucinda would discover it like oil in a well and was sure to turn the story loose. Coworkers put a new twist on the old joke about the three most effective ways of mass communication: Telegraph, telephone, tell a woman. Now it was simply, Tell Lucinda. Emma had been forewarned of Lucinda's reputation when she started working at FAC three years ago.

Emma used to work at reception with Lucinda but was promoted after studying business and advertising part-time at Mercy Springs Community College. She finally graduated with her associate's degree and was promoted. Hard work and sassy ideas on client projects helped.

She always tried to keep on everyone's good side. As much as possible.

"Please, have a seat." Evan leaned back in the executive leather chair in the boardroom as he gestured to the chair nearest him. His voice was deep, low. Sexy.

God, he was stunning.

His arresting good looks sure cranked up Emma's heart rate. She'd worked with him for three years, and he never ceased to have that effect on her. His dark, sensual brown eyes, chiselled cheekbones and dimpled smile were a definite turn-on for her. Dark, healthy, wavy hair that made you wish you could run your fingers through it.

And his body? Though he sported a business suit, Emma could not ignore his tall, muscular physique. He worked out hard at the gym as much as he worked diligently at the office. A sure catch. Unattached by sheer choice. Not that all the women in the office didn't throw themselves at him. He'd been known to have affluent dates, from society elites, to actresses, models, and heiresses, but commitment just was not his thing and he made that known. Emma didn't even try to compete. She wouldn't know where to begin. She kept her mad crush on him a private and confidential secret.

"Sorry I'm late." She flushed.

The graphic designer, art director, and two account coordinators sat around the oak boardroom table waiting for the conference call from Weddings R Us. It was new corporation that will open a record twenty stores across the U.S. in the next year. They were already a huge success in Canada. A one-stop shopping for all your bridal needs for all budgets. Kind of like having your own wedding planner for a fraction of the cost. They also handled bookings for receptions, pre-marriage counselling, attire, decorations, cakes, the whole works. The seven-figure deal would be the largest for Fletcher Advertising and Emma knew Evan had her in mind to head the account with him.

During the conference meeting, thirty-three-year-old Evan stole discreet glances at his beautiful employee, Emma. She looked much younger than her thirty years. He loved her simple, yet chic, dress style. She rarely followed fads, knew what colors complemented her sweet, honey complexion and what styles accentuated her natural curves. He loved her silhouette. He didn't think there was anything not to like about her. He tried to divert his eyes from her gorgeous toned legs as she crossed them to the side.

If Emma Wiggins were any hotter she'd be a fire hazard, he mused.

He could also sense she was preoccupied. Maybe he should have given her leave knowing that her grandfather was ill. Evan truly didn't know how ill he was.

But this was a huge deal and Fletcher Advertising couldn't afford to blow it. Evan admired Emma. She was the best. He knew this would be ideal for her career, too.

Still, he admired more than just her brains. He often imagined her and him together in... It was just a fantasy, he dismissed the thought as quickly as it entered his mind. Men were allowed to fantasize once in a while. But he wouldn't dare let on to his employee he had those thoughts about her. She was young, but at the age where she deserved a man who believed in commitment. Evan could never, even if he wanted to, commit to any woman.

He'd learned his lesson the hard way. It almost destroyed him on many levels. His career. His business. His health.

Fletcher men and marriage didn't mix.

Or else, the consequences could be...

Evan didn't want to entertain that thought now. He had to keep his reserve of positive energy flowing. He didn't know why he was drawn to Emma, but he was more drawn to keeping his sanity in tact and his business away from another potential scandal.

She was an employee.

Nothing more.

An hour later after the conference call ended, Evan pressed the release button on the phone.

"Nice work, team." He was buoyed and cheered his group on. The initial pitch went well. They would present to Weddings R Us in person tomorrow when the execs from New York reached town.

Evan drove his team hard but commended them for their efforts. He was a fair boss and a team player, but everyone knew how to hold their own. He wasn't someone who tolerated poor excuses or failure. But he was there if you were willing to put out the effort.

As everyone left the meeting, Evan, who had been eyeing, Emma told her to stay back.

"Is everything okay, Emma? How's your grandfather doing?" Evan admired how Emma worked conscientiously at the firm and gave it her all. He also loved her tenacity and commitment to taking care of her grandfather. He knew she spent a great deal of time at the hospital visiting him. In fact, when her car conked out he'd given her a ride to the long-term care facility a few times.

"Oh, he—"

"Sorry, Emma, you have an urgent call from the hospital." Lucinda bolted through the door of the boardroom and told her the call was on line one.

Emma looked as if her heart stopped.

"Emma, do you need me to stay?" Evan offered, a look of concern befalling his face.

Relief swept over her tensed shoulders. "Actually, sure…if you don't mind." She seemed breathless.

Oh, no. Is he dead? And I wasn't even there by his side. Emma had planned to leave work earlier today—which meant on time-to go back to the hospital to visit her grandfather.

"Hi, Emma. This is Petra, your grandfather's nurse."

"Yes?" She sounded too sharp, anxious at first. She must have come across way too strong. She could picture the look on the face of the redhead nurse with the bright pink uniform.

"Nothing to worry about. It's just that your grandfather's condition has…well, changed slightly."

"What do you mean? Is he okay?" Panic rose in Emma's chest. She was conscious of Evan's concern and his warm energy flowing her direction. She was thankful for his support.

"Well, yes. You see, when you left, he perked up. He started eating again. He had more energy. The doctor was saying that he probably had more than days. More like weeks. It's not unusual for some patients to get a sudden burst of energy. We call it the Hope Factor. Sometimes a wave of hope keeps their spirit going a little longer. A lost relative on their way to see them after all these years. Things like that. Sometimes they hold on until whatever they're waiting for comes to pass."

"Oh, thank God." Emma sighed a deep sigh of relief as she expelled a whiff of suppressed air. She didn't realize she had held her breath.

"Oh, and congratulations!"

"For?"

"On your engagement."

Uh-oh!

"My what?" Emma's brain activity fired up all kinds of thoughts. She wondered if the news of her fake impending marriage had anything to do with her grandfather's topped up spirit—his second wind of hope. Just then, a sick feeling sank inside her stomach. She could not bring herself to peer into Evan's concerned, unsuspecting face. He had no idea what was going on.

"Right. Of course." Emma swallowed, ever aware of Evan's soft, sexy brown eyes on her.

"By the way, the reason why I'm calling now is because your grandfather is so excited about you getting married that he's spoken with the chaplain at the hospital. The end of next week would be fine to have the ceremony here. We can have the wedding take place in your grandfather's room. We just need to get the groom's name.

Is that Evan Fletcher spelled E-V-A-N F-L-E-T-C-H-E-R.?"

What?

Emma froze.

The phone pressed firmly to her ear, she could not move or blink or breathe.

Oh, God, help me! Now, what have I done?

"Not to pry, but is everything okay, Emma? You don't look too well." Evan leaned in closer to her as if he were ready to catch her fall as she stood looking as if she would pass out any minute by the side table.

She was clearly in a daze.

The look of shock—or was that horror--glazed over her face. Evan looked aghast as if she was having a cardiac arrest and he needed to do something—quick!

"Um..." She could barely speak. But she had to say something.

Oh, Lord. Now what have I gotten myself—and my boss— into?

3

Two hours later, Emma sat typing away at her keyboard on her desk. They were on tight deadline to get the presentation pitch ready for the principals at Weddings R Us.

She hated herself for telling that fib earlier in the day. The lie about her engagement to Evan. Now, she hated herself even more. How was she going to wiggle out of this one?

Her brain was working overtime. A thousand thoughts a minute. How was she going to impress her new potential client? And how was she going to convince Evan to go along with marrying her next week, for the sake of her dear old dying grandfather.

Stupid. Stupid. Stupid.

Why did you have to open up your big mouth? You should've just listened and not said anything. Now you have to get married next week. Or else.

"Got a second?" Evan poked his head around her opened door, causing Emma to jolt upright with a flush on her face.

SHADONNA RICHARDS

"Sure, Evan. Anything." Her cheeks burned. Her insides felt like a hundreds of butterflies had turned loose inside her belly.

I need air. I need Evan.

"Okay, I've got the sketch for the new ad design. I thought we could go with a touch of tradition and a blend of new age."

"Sounds great. I also think we should add in the multicultural mix. Give it the universal appeal. You know the effect."

He nodded, stroking his chin. "Good, good. But we need to design a fresh angle. Remember, they're eyeing a few agencies for their big campaign."

"Yeah, but we're in their top two."

"Soon to be number one."

They both smiled. For a moment, Emma's brown eyes locked with Evan's deep, rich dark eyes. She quivered inside. She had to remind herself who he was. Her boss. Her very serious-minded, all business, commitment-phobic boss who also held the keys to her promotion. Her dream was to one day head the department as Account Director. Evan was already in the process of giving her a wonderful reference to get into the master's program for business admin to which she was eternally grateful.

What could she do? Should she deliver the news of their impending marriage? Or risk breaking her dying grandfather's heart by telling him she fabricated the whole marriage thing?

"Um…Evan. Just wondering. You know. About our new potential client."

"What about them?"

"Weddings R Us. What is your take on…you know…weddings?"

"Well, I haven't hidden the fact how I feel about marriage. Not into it. Not for me. But of course, that's between us. We can't have Weddings R Us thinking I don't believe in their product now, can we?" His facial expression and body language spoke volumes. You would think he was asked about shaving off his scalp as an experiment by the look of disgust in his cringed facial expression.

"So you would never consider marriage?" she asked, a teensy bit of hope edging her query.

"Never." Evan's brows furrowed. "Emma, why are you asking me this now?"

Now it was Emma's turn to be tongue-tied. "Oh, um…nothing. It's just that. Well, we need to believe in our client's work and…" She swallowed hard. *Where are you going with this thing, stupid? You're digging yourself in deeper. Shut up and quit while you can. Quit talking.* But she couldn't help herself. She had to find a way to discuss getting married next week or face smashing her dying grandfather's heart in a million tiny pieces. The latter seemed more unbearable at the moment.

Evan couldn't help but notice Emma's strange behaviour. He wondered what she was hiding. He didn't take too well to people keeping secrets. Especially those he trusted.

Still, he had to respect her privacy. He figured it was the stress of caring for an ill relative.

Lord knows he could relate to that. His own father was his responsibility—which reminded him. The home-visit nurse had called earlier to tell him that his father refused his medication again. He was going over there to pay a quick visit. That meant he would be leaving the office earlier than usual, then coming back later in the evening to finish up the proposal for the potential new client.

Talk about timing.

"Hey, listen." Evan grew impatient and the thought of his father colored his mood in an unfavourable way. "Outside of the client, the subject of marriage or weddings is off." It seemed as if the serious look he directed towards Emma caused her heart to stop. He noticed she swallowed hard.

"Sure. No more mention of weddings. Outside of the office, so to speak. Let's get down to business." She laughed nervously. What was with her? She was usually so calm, collected, in control. Not now. Not around Evan. And not after that ridiculous could-kick-herself-a-thousand-times-for-that-stupid-little-indescretion moment she had at the hospital today. All because she was trying to spare her Gramps's feelings as he lay helplessly, in the last few days—or weeks—of his life.

"Good." Evan did not look back up at Emma. She didn't know how to take that. Still he was irresistible. The scent of his aftershave drove her crazy. His clean shaven, honey-tanned skinned reigned smooth enough to stroke. But she dared not. Why did she keep having these recurrent thoughts of her boss?

He was, after all, her boss. And so completely, irrevocably, unavailable.

Stop it. Stop it. Focus, Emma. Focus. Okay, so the issue of bringing up getting married next week is out of the question. Good thing I've always got a plan B.

She watched as he spread out pages of information and pored over them. Different pieces of ideas from the graphics department were included for the full picture. They mulled over which spread to present at their big client meeting tomorrow.

Emma thought five o'clock would never come.

She logged out, switched off her computer, and grabbed her keys and handbag. She was satisfied with the materials and ideas she presented to Evan for their upcoming client meeting. Now, she had to settle another issue. At the hospital. Her fake wedding that she must stop. If only it was as simple as hitting the escape key on the computer.

Later that evening, Evan pulled up to the ranch where his father lived. The housekeeper, June, was usually in the back doing laundry at this hour.

Memories of their once happy home that was filled with music and laughter faded with each step. It had been ten years since the messy divorce that flipped his father's world upside down. His own mother died when he was born. He never knew her outside of the photos stored in the attic. His step-mother, his father's second wife, banished the pictures when she was Mrs. Evan Fletcher, Senior. But she left. The pictures came down from the attic. It was hard on his father dealing with his mother's death at childbirth. Then his second wife walking out on him in the scandal that almost rocked this side of Mercy Springs, Texas. But Evan could not think about that now. He was paying for a private nurse to come in to see his father every so now and again, but twenty-four hour care may be the way to go. If he secured the deal with Weddings R Us, that may be more feasible.

Evan walked up the cobblestone pathway to the house. He could hear the TV blared to full volume and the stereo on high.

"Dad, what are you doing?" Evan walked briskly over to the TV and turned down the volume. "Where's June?"

June rushed in, her face flushed, her eyes on the verge of tears. "He's been climbing the walls again. You should see the kitchen. He keeps saying the devil is in the house, and he's going to chase him out by cranking up the volume." June threw her hands up and her head back.

"What have I gotten myself into? I can't take any more, Evan. He needs to go away."

"No." Evan's anger rose fierce. "My father's not going into some home."

June knew too well that when Evan, Jr. didn't want to do something, it wasn't going to be done. Once he'd made up his mind, that was that. His Royal Stubbornness inherited the trait from his father. But June was a distant cousin and more family than help.

"It's the curse! The curse!" His father came back from the kitchen with a broom in his hand. "The Fletcher curse. Evan, don't ever fall in love. Women. They'll steal your mind, steal your heart, and steal your soul. The curse."

"Dad. Okay, enough. Stop it now." Evan tried to be as gentle yet firm with his father as possible. The transition was almost enough to break his strong spirit. This man who taught him everything he knew about life, love, business. Ethics. Once a strong man. Prominent business man in the community. Reduced to an emotionally fragile state of pity.

"What's this about the curse? The Fletcher curse, Evan? That's new."

At first, Evan ignored June and convinced his father to take his anti-psychotic medication. "Dad, you need to take your medicine to help you feel better. Remember what the doctor said?"

"Oh, Evan. When did you get here? Nice to see you again." The elder Mr. Fletcher extended his hand to be shaken.

By now, Evan's eyes moistened. Not something June was used to seeing. She knew it must be hard for Evan. He loved his father and this must have been torture for him. Finally, the elder Fletcher took his pills and sipped a cup of water, like a child, defenceless, harmless. No, Evan would not like to see his father institutionalized.

Somehow, the elder Fletcher would listen to his son, though not always to the home visit staff that saw him from time to time.

Evan knew how important compliance with medication was for his father as an outpatient. To remain as an outpatient. And even if that meant coming back and forth, driving from south Mercy Springs to north Mercy Springs to where his father's ranch was located ten times a day-so be it.

Evan got back to June on her question. "The Fletcher curse is not new, June. Dad told me about it when I was much younger. But it was meant to be secret."

June stood silently, her mop still in her hand. She'd cleaned up the spill in the kitchen earlier after the elder Fletcher thought he saw the "devil in a cape hiding in the kitchen" and wanted to "wash him out with ice water."

Evan drew in a deep breath and bit down on his lip. "Grandpa took a rifle to his head back in the day. It wasn't because he lost everything in the depression. It was…because of a woman. And Dad, well…" He broke off.

"It's okay, Evan. It's okay. You don't have to go into it."

"I'm good. I'll be fine. I guess that's why I'm not exactly gung ho on this marriage business. I mean, it doesn't seem to agree with the Fletcher men, does it? Then there was great-grandpa who did the same thing. It's like commitment leads to being committed." He chuckled a humorless laugh, trying to bury his own memory of having his heart broken. "Seems like the Fletcher men have a curse of loving too hard and falling too hard if it doesn't work out."

Still, Evan thought about it. He had another problem he didn't wish to think about right now. It had something to do with keeping as far away from the beautiful Emma Wiggins as much as he could handle it.

4

"Here she comes, the beautiful bride-to-be." Grandpa Wiggins smiled broadly when Emma approached him at the hospital. He was sitting up in the wheelchair, his friend Mr. Harry at his side along with Mr. Harry's visitor.

"Gramps, you're looking so well. Hi, Mr. H." Emma greeted both her grandfather and his buddy. It appeared they were playing cards. What a change from earlier when she thought he had mere days to live.

Emma swallowed.

This was not going to be easy for her. She had to tell him somehow, that the wedding he was looking forward to—wouldn't be happening any time soon. She wished she had support now. She wished she could talk it over with someone she could trust. But who? Outside of her former roommate, college study-buddy, and neighbour, Genie, she had no one. But Genie was probably on a hot date and Emma needed to talk, and she needed to do it, like now. Never had she felt so alone.

Just then, her phone buzzed. She glanced and was shocked to see her mother's number on the display.

She hadn't spoken to her mother in months. Her mother moved to Toronto years ago with her new boyfriend. They weren't exactly bosom buddies—though she wished things were different between them. They just didn't see eye-to-eye on much. Her parents never got along. Her mother was the younger woman and her father was years her senior, still Emma clung more to the Wiggins side of the family. To Emma, Gramps was her closest living relative now.

Just as she reached to press the talk button, her grandfather touched her hand. "Darling, I forgot to mention. I got in touch with your mother today. She was shocked but excited about you getting married. She and her new beau will be here next week. Is Friday good for you? Figured better sooner than later. You know, like Mr. H here. The wedding was beautiful, wasn't it?" Her grandfather spewed out the words, then he turned to his friend whom he often refers to as Mr. H.

Emma stopped cold. She could not answer the call. Not now. How on earth was she going to tell her mother that she lied, too? A sick thought struck Emma at that moment. She was afraid to part her lips to speak, but she quickly worked through that crippling fear. "Um, Gramps. Just who else did you tell about the wedding?" She tried to sound as casual as possible. Cool and level voiced, though she just wasn't sure how convincing she was. Mr. H excused himself to walk his visitor to the door. Sometimes, Emma could not believe this was a long-term care palliative unit where the residents had months or weeks to live. They didn't all seem to be at death's door, at least apparently not to the naked, medically untrained eye.

"Oh, just the family, dear." He leaned back in his wheelchair with a self-satisfied grin. It was plastered on the same face that earlier looked as if the life had been drained from it. Right now, Emma felt the life was draining from her whole being.

"The family?"

"Yes, your mother and her beau. Cousin Lucy. Mark. David. Mavis."

Emma's face fell. "What? Gramps!"

"What darling?" He looked concerned and stopped rocking. "I thought it would be nice, darling."

He leaned closer to his granddaughter who sat kneeling on the floor beside his chair. "Darling, when you reach my age and at the stage where I am, there isn't much to look forward to. I'm so glad that you and this Evan fellow are getting married. This has given me such a peace and a joy I can't explain." His eyes watered.

"I just don't want everyone to gather together only when I'm gone. Isn't it better to celebrate while we still have breath in our lungs?" he continued as he held her shoulder. "I'm sure your mother would be here for my funeral. But I won't see her then. Hadn't seen her and the family since I don't know when. I wanna celebrate life. A new beginning. And, Emma, I can't tell you how proud I am of you. I'm glad you moved on after what that other guy did to you. I'm so glad you're getting married and bringing the family together."

Tears trickled down his face. Emma felt sick to her stomach over her web of deceit, her face flushed. She grabbed a tissue from the Kleenex box and gently wiped his cheeks. She needed one for her own tears, too.

She was surreptitiously mourning the death of the woman she would become. Her life was so over as she knew it. She couldn't argue with her grandfather as to his sentiments. He was so right. God, why did she lie about getting married to Evan Fletcher? Evan! Her boss! Now how on earth was she going to pull this off?

She couldn't kill off her grandfather with a crippling shock that she'd lied about everything. She just couldn't snatch hope out of a dying man's heart. No way. Neither could she destroy commitment-phobic Evan, her boss, with a commitment he had no part in consenting to.

How on earth was the ever-so-resourceful Emma Wiggins going to wiggle her way out of this one? It was Monday evening, she had less than eleven days to get married to Evan or risk ruining her life and that of everyone she cared about.

Emma scooted up the stairwell to her apartment—she didn't have the patience to wait for the elevator that was forever stuck on the twelfth floor. The other elevator was on service. Probably a new tenant moving in. It was a new development building in the southern part of Mercy Springs just off Peach Street. She loved the architecture of the place and couldn't help admiring every corner of the building every time she walked through the doors.

She opted out of taking the elevator in the twelve-story building to walk up to the fifth floor. She needed to let off stream, to blow off some of that adrenalin that had her going all day. The stairwell had windows going up so residents could see outside. Not a bad security feature, she mused. She peered out as she continued up the steps with her bag swinging off her shoulder and thoughts of Evan Fletcher swimming in her brain. She just couldn't get him off her mind. Truth was, she dreamed of him, fantasized about him, lusted for him—day and night. She'd always had this mad crush on him and now...That crush, which materialized into a full-blown lie based on a fantasy, could very well ruin everything she'd worked so hard for. When she blurted out to her grandfather that she was seeing someone, she hadn't counted on him asking her the name of that mysterious gentleman. Of course, the fact that Evan was always on her mind and the subject of her many inner thoughts and deep desires surfaced. His name naturally came to mind. Surreptitiously, she'd wished they could be an item—but for professional and now personal reasons, that truly couldn't work out.

Funny, how the biggest lies we tell are to ourselves. She probably sublimated her fantasies and really believed for just that instant that she and Evan were engaged and getting married. Now, she all she had to do was come up with a plan that would work.

It was late in the evening, the moon was full against the dark sky, and the building seemed quiet until she arrived at her floor. The sound of her heels rendered a muffled trumping sound on the carpet of the hallway leading to her apartment. She could hear the television sets blaring from a few units going towards her unit. Jazz music blasted out of number 504, the door next to her own.

"Yep, Genie's home, alright." She was glad her best friend and former roommate was home. She could hear muted talking and giggles amidst the music. It appeared Genie may have been either on the phone or with someone. She didn't want to intrude but took a chance and gave a light tap on the door with her keys for a greater effect.

"Just a minute," she heard Genie yell from beyond the door.

She saw a shadow pass across the peep hole and knew Genie had looked to see who was knocking at this hour. When Emma glanced at her watch, she realized it was ten o'clock. Not too terribly late. She had stayed later past the hospital's nine o'clock visiting hours to be with her grandfather. She didn't realize it was that late.

"Only me, hon!" She winked knowing Genie could see her through the peep hole. Emma heard the clanking of the chain being unhooked on the other side and the door swung open.

"Hey, girl. What's up?" Genie had a drink in her hand and her cordless in the other.

"Oh, sorry, I didn't mean to intrude. Are you busy?"

"Girl, I've always got time for you. Don't be silly."

Emma really appreciated Genie's openness and friendship. In college it was a two-way street. She'd helped Genie many nights with her tough subjects like English and Comp. In fact, she'd written many of her essays and tutored her on the language since English was Genie's second language. Genie was eternally grateful and in turn would help Emma with other essentials like savvy shopping for the best deals. When the new development was built, they rushed to get in on the builder's deals. Genie's uncle bought a few units and rented them out to students. They both lucked out and rented the available units that were side-by-side. She used to think it would be a curse living that close to her best friend. What if she didn't feel in the mood to talk or go out or just wanted some quiet time? Something she craved a lot. But it turned out to be a blessing in disguise. Genie was back in school part-time and had an incredibly busy social life with tons of friends outside of their own friendship. She was loyal and discreet.

Genie eyed Emma up quickly as she pulled the door wide open. "Just got in from work?"

"Oh, yeah!" Emma walked in and saw books scattered everywhere. There were posters and loose papers on the floor, shoes and blankets scattered everywhere. She noticed a box of pizza on the center coffee table that had been pushed to the side along with empty cans of pop. Seemed like Genie had a study party earlier, or some form of fun. Genie told the person on the phone that she'd call her back later. Genie had on a shorts and midriff t-shirt. Ever the teen-at-heart, though she was twenty-nine. She could easily pass for a teen. She had a rough life and pretty much raised herself. She once told Emma, now was her time to reclaim her youth and live for the moment. Have fun while bettering herself. She dreamed of owning her own business one day.

"Can I get you anything?"

"Oh, I'm good, thanks. Just visited Gramps and we ate at the hospital."

Genie's expression turned sympathetic. "Aw! How is old man Wiggins doing?"

"He's good. You know, so much has happened today. First, as you know, the docs told me that he didn't have much time," Emma recounted as she sat with Genie on the sofa crowded with overstuffed teddies and large colourful pillows. "Well, now they say he has weeks to live. Maybe another two. They can't be sure." Emma bit down on her lip and tried to fight back tears. She fiddled with the zip of her imitation Gucci handbag.

Genie sighed and embraced her friend. For a moment they both sat hugging. Emma felt guilty for barging in and ranting about her day. "How's your studying coming along?"

"It's good. Not bad. Got another presentation to give for my elective. God, I hate those." The two women giggled. "But enough about class. I wanna forget about that for tonight. I've been busting my brain all day trying to get this project going. I know you didn't come to chat at this hour about my class."

"C'mon, Gene."

"No, really, there's something else on your mind. I can tell, girl, you don't fool me."

"Well, you're right." At first Emma hesitated. Sometimes she found it necessary to censor herself with friends in fear of looking like a fool, but then she reminded herself she was talking with her best friend for life, or as was all the rage to say, her BFF. Her non-judgemental girlfriend on whom she could always count.

Emma sighed deeply and spilled everything to Genie. The uncut, uncensored, utterly ridiculous version.

The whole shebang. She needed to vent. She needed support or she'd burst at the emotional seams.

After Emma's spiel, Genie sat wide-eyed and mouth agape.

Emma squirmed slightly, feeling foolish. "Well, aren't you going to say anything?"

Genie clasped her hand over her forehead, shaking her head. "Okay, so let me get this straight. You told your grandfather you were going to marry Evan Fletcher, the president of Fletcher Advertising? Your boss? The one who hates women?"

"Hey, he doesn't hate women!" Emma interjected as she rolled her eyes and shook her head. "He just doesn't believe in…you know…commitment."

"Right." Genie got up, sighed, and paced like a detective on a mission to solve a case. "So, you pretty much allowed your grandfather, who is dying, to believe that you are going to marry your boss and he made arrangements for you two to get hitched next week." Genie's tone was light and humorous but she was trying to be supportive to her best friend who really got herself into a pickle this time. She remembered when she was in a bind, many times and Emma bailed her out without so much as a hushed whisper.

"Emma, I should have told you this before, but during my psych class, I studied phobias really well."

"And?"

"Well, you remember the term—gamophobia?"

"Gamo--? No way."

"Yes, way. Gamophobia is a word from the Greek term 'gamete' meaning wife and 'gamein' which means—"

"To marry," Emma finished for her.

"Evan Fletcher is gamophobic," Genie continued, "That crap is for real and it ain't funny."

"Gamophobia," Emma smacked her hand over her forehead and slouched back into the cushiony couch, chuckling humorlessly. "An anxiety disorder for those who fear the responsibility of marriage or even living with someone."

"He fits the description to a tee, girl. Of all the men in Texas you had to force to marry. You had to choose Mr. Marriage-will-cause-my-head-to-explode phobia." Genie couldn't help but stifle a giggle and rubbed Emma's shoulder.

"Great, I remember that project we did back in college." Emma recounted all too well. The symptoms of panic attacks, heart palpitations, shortness of breath, dry mouth. She noticed when she bought up the whole marriage thing to sexy, capable Evan, he flinched. Seemed like every man had a weakness of some sort.

Suddenly, Emma felt sick to her stomach. She had deep feelings for Evan, and she thought she caught him undressing her with his eyes when he thought her back was completely turned on occasion, but now she was beginning to think it was her imagination. They had a huge contract to clinch tomorrow. He was probably at the office hard at work. If they sealed the deal—that would mean flying off to New York the following week to shoot the first commercial. How on earth was she going to get this wedding thing going and even bring up the idea of marriage to him—thanks to her oversized gob? Was she seriously considering this? She could not risk him getting into a serious fit over this. Going back to Gramps was also out of the question.

"Well, every problem has a solution, girl," Genie interrupted Emma's mental guilt trip. "Your mouth got your into this, so your mouth's gonna get you *out* of it."

The look of disbelief splashed across Emma's flushed face as she shook her head and rolled her eyes. "And how do you propose I do *that*, Einstein?"

Genie gave Emma a sly grin. "Are you gonna listen to my plan, or not?"

Emma sighed. Did she really have a choice?

5

Evan paced in angst over the mock storyboard for the advertising pitch.

It was Tuesday morning—the thunder rolled hard outside as the rain poured on this April spring morning. That afternoon would be his monumental chance to win the Weddings R Us account and contract for the big launch.

He walked over to the lounge area in the two-story loft on the fourth floor of the glass building that housed Fletcher Advertising. It spanned the entire fourth floor. The design of the loft was creative yet subtle. It had the residential appeal with a corporate environment. A plush couch sat in the reception area with tall green plants, art décor on the wall. Evan enjoyed the open space concept. Offices were on one side of the loft with glass doors and windows. Blinds covered most of the area for privacy. A conference room and boardroom also existed. He had carefully selected the décor on purpose for an environment conducive to art, creativity, and relaxation. In other words, he despised the stuffy corporate offices where he used to work, and he wanted a more stress-free, cosy work environment in downtown Mercy Springs. At that moment, he felt anything but stress-free.

Last night, Evan, along with a few members of the team, including Emma who gave her input and got down to work on the mock ads to present in the pitch, spent hours ploughing over the sample print and TV ad storyboards. He was pleased with the efforts but wanted to make sure he missed nothing.

This meant a lot for his business and his personal life. He would be able to propel Fletcher Advertising further in the industry and take care of his father the way he wanted to by hiring a private duty nurse for twenty-four hour supervision.

Still, he couldn't get the thought of his adorable yet complex account coordinator, Emma, out of his mind. Boy, he wished he could figure her out. The scent of her sweet perfume was always a distraction for him. It was a sugary, baby scent that drove him wild. He dared not ask her the name of it. But he figured it was one of the popular designer perfumes.

Keep your mind focused, Evan.

Still, all this talk of weddings started to nudge him. He grabbed his espresso from the table and slurped the remainder down as he held on to the artwork from his up-and-coming artist in the other hand. The copywriter worked closely with Emma to get the slogan just right.

Emma had called him early this morning to let him know she had a breakthrough with a better slogan—and that she would be in a tad later in the morning. He didn't mind since she had worked late at night from home after visiting her grandfather at the hospital. He had asked her about her grandfather and was glad to learn he was doing much better. He wished he could say the same about his father.

He sighed.

He was eager to hear about Emma's idea on the pitch this morning. He loved the concept. He couldn't wait to see what she had printed out from her computer at home. Evan really appreciated when his staff, especially Emma, went the extra mile.

Evan didn't require his employees to work from home, but Emma had a raw dedication he admired. She cared about her work. She took pride in meeting the needs of their clients. It was all about meeting needs. Solving problems for society—one step at a time. Every thought she put behind her words and her work had the interest of the betterment of others. If she didn't feel it was worth it or fair, she would state her claim.

God, he loved her spunk. They seemed to, oddly, have a great deal in common. They both loved soccer—and she had suggested they have a company team last year. That went very well. They played his rival advertising agency and beat them 4-2. What a game!

He always told her she "could kick ass without moving a foot." And he was right. She was smooth and swift but to the point on an argument. Any argument.

Whenever they had to eat out or order take-out when working late at the office—which was becoming a habit lately—she knew exactly what he wanted to order and what food he was in the mood for on a given day which changed every so now and again. It was as if she knew him as well as she knew herself. Was she studying his habits? Or him, perhaps?

But lately, she seemed to be preoccupied. Probably had to do with her grandfather.

Okay, Evan, enough already. Why are you thinking about Emma so much?

With his hands shoved his pockets of his tailored blue suit, he moved away from his desk and walked over to the passageway to get a glimpse of the weather outside at the full wall to wall, ceiling to floor window. He often dressed down on a day-to-day basis, but when there was a client pitch or business meeting, he was all business. His Armani suits spoke volumes that he was a true professional.

The view of south Mercy Springs was breathtaking. He could see the beautiful lake to the side and the backdrop of Mercy Springs. The hills in the background, the view of the downtown core. The traffic below.

He had an unobstructed view of the street and could see people coming in and out of the building. The rain was letting up slightly and the grey clouds were beginning to lighten by the minute. He had to think of something besides his account coordinator. He would focus on the Weddings R Us account. Visualize winning the contract. The company had already given him the heads-up that they had shortlisted two ad agencies including Fletcher Advertising for the deal. Now, it was up to them.

"Oh, great!"

Just then, he caught a glimpse of Emma walking across the street. She looked stunning in her trench coat as it flapped open. She wore a peach dress with a plunging neckline that was cut above her knee. Her bosoms heaved as she strode across the street towards the glass building. Her hoop earrings, dangling fashion necklace, and scarf accentuated her features. She was always so coordinated from hairline to her pedicured toes. Her long, curly ebony hair shined as it swayed almost rhythmically from side to side with the gentle spring breeze. She oozed confidence. Grace. Beauty. Charisma. He hated to sound cliché, but she looked as if she was one of those models in a hair or clothing commercial. Evan felt his privates tingle. He was embarrassed by his feelings and had to shift his focus. She was, after all, his employee. Nothing more. Besides, even if things were different, he was not the commitment type. But he wasn't going down that road again.

Maybe looking out the window was not such a good idea after all.

He stretched, got back to his desk, leaned back in his leather chair, and continued to mull over finishing details of his pitch.

Emma rushed into the office with her bag and materials for the presentation that afternoon.

She had risen early at 4 o'clock in the morning to put her mock print ad together along with her slogans.

Little did Evan know she had two pitches lined up. One for the client and the other for him. She was still working out in her mind the latter.

Landing this hot account meant a lot to FAC as well as to Emma. She tried to push the thoughts of yesterday morning out of her mind—but she kept Genie's wacky idea in mind. If her own plan or wedding pitch to Evan failed, she would have to follow Genie's advice.

She shuddered at the thought.

"Oh, Emma. There's a meeting at 10:30 in the boardroom," Lucinda called out as Emma hurried past the reception desk.

"Oh, right. Thanks." Emma tried to hide her disappointment that the practice pitch was scheduled so early. She was hoping she would have a little more time to herself before meeting and going over last minute ideas.

Emma lugged her backpack and papers into her office. Everything all seemed so surreal. This would have been an ordinary day at the office if it hadn't been for the huge gaffe she sputtered out yesterday. But she had to push that to the back of her mind for the moment.

She pulled off her trench coat and wiggled to pull down her dress that had ridden up—when she turned around to close the door, she froze. Evan stood at the door with his hand partially raised about to knock.

She thought she saw him flush—but that had to be her imagination.

"Sorry, er, if I caught you at a bad time." Evan tried hard not to look directly at Emma's thighs. He shuffled some papers in his hand and handed her a sheet. "What do you think?"

It was a briefing with some statistics on weddings.

"Great. Um…" Emma fixed her dress and stood erect as she grabbed the sheet of paper from Evan.

She felt breathless, but she tried to hide it. Evan looked ravishing in his dark blue, executive suit. God, did he look delicious enough to eat.

Stop it, Emma. Focus.

As her eyes quickly ran down the page of information on their new client meeting, she felt Evan's eyes scan her own silhouette. Or was that her imagination? She glanced up quickly.

Nope, it was not her imagination. Their eyes locked momentarily. This was so awkward. Yep, he definitely blushed. For a second, his sexy, dark brown eyes pierced into her. His eyes travelled down, he blushed then looked away. She glanced down at the sheet but was horrified to see that her cleavage was showing a little more than she had intended. Oh, great. She had purchased the lycra cotton fabric spring dress, but hadn't worn it until today. When she had readjusted her dress, that wasn't the only part of the dress that went south. He cleared his throat and changed the non-verbal subject.

"So? Do you think we should go ahead with the stats during the meeting for more persuasive effect?" He transformed his expression to all-business. She could tell he was slightly embarrassed. Probably more than she was, if that were at all possible.

"Um. Definitely." She tried hard not to be distracted by the scent of his sweet aftershave and his presence. It was definitely hard to focus. "I think we should go ahead and throw in all we've got. Let them know we've done our research above and beyond."

"Great. Well, why don't you look these over? I'll leave these with you. See you in twenty."

"Right. Oh, and Evan."

"Yes?" He turned around with his hands in his pockets. God, he looked irresistible. His shirt and black tie made him look so sophisticated. Though he had on his suit, you could tell he had a killer body underneath it. His biceps were ripped. He stood firm. Erect. Confident. Fit at six feet, four inches.

"Um…" She needed to talk to him today, after the meeting. Hopefully if all went well with the pitch. "I was just wondering, if-"

"Evan, Bianca is on line one." Just then, Lucinda walked by with her headset in her ear; she had left the reception desk to deliver the news.

"Oh, I'll be right there. Keep her on hold."

Okay, so who is this Bianca, again? Emma racked her brain to try to remember where she heard the name before. *A client? No. Family? No. Oh. My. God. His ex? What does she want?*

Emma tried to hide the panic in her expression. This could only complicate things, but for starters, he would normally tell Lucinda he would call the person back. Oh, God. Were they getting back together? She wished she could pry into his private business right now. If only it were appropriate.

Okay, calm down, Emma. Don't go jumping to conclusion. Keep it professional.

"Yes, you were saying?" Evan turned back to Emma as he derailed her secret panic attack.

"Um. Oh, right. Yes, I was wondering if…" *after the meeting today, you'll considering marrying me next week before we go to New York?* "…we could speak after the meeting today." Emma was a bundle of nerves inside. She hoped he didn't see or notice the quiver in her voice. The falsetto. Her unusual higher pitch of tone.

"Oh, of course. Is everything okay?" He wrinkled his brow. A look of concern on his face made Emma realize he could think it was a more serious issue—but then again, maybe it was.

"Well, yes, it's fine. I, well, I just needed to talk to you about…" *ruining your life while I try to convert you from a carefree bachelor to an overnight groom.* "…something important, that's all. Nothing to do with work." *Okay, that may not have come out right.*

Evan shot Emma a puzzled look but shrugged. "Sure. I'm game. After the meeting." He sighed. "Thanks again for your hard work and all the time you've put in on this. I really appreciate it."

"Thanks, Evan. I know you do. And thanks for having me on this team. Let's get 'em." Emma threw a team punch as she winked—trying way too hard to keep her nerves under control. *Okay that sounded lame, but I'm trying to hide the insanity that will later overtake me.*

This had better work, Emma thought to herself. But, first things first. She had to give it all she had for the pitch this afternoon. She sighed as she walked over to her desk, sat, and leaned back into her leather chair.

Emma made sure the boardroom was booked for the pitch at 2:30 p.m. and that the caterers were coming to deliver the refreshments for the meeting.

She had picked out some of the client's favorites. She'd always gone to great lengths to do her due diligence ahead of time and ensure every client felt right at home when they arrived at Fletcher Advertising.

She checked and rechecked to assure the décor in the boardroom suited that of a wedding reception or luncheon. She ordered pastries and wine in addition to fresh fruits, cocktails, and lined the chairs with wedding satin chair covers. Matching silk and cream coloured balloons adorned the boardroom. It looked exquisite.

"I'm impressed." Evan smiled as he walked into the boardroom with the copywriter, graphic designer, and account executive. They had brainstormed earlier and decided to go with a full theme to celebrate Weddings R Us. Over by the wall, hung a poster with a list: 10 Reasons Why Every Bride Needs Weddings R Us. Followed by a list of the top ten reasons adding some valuable tips in addition to marital humor and various union scenarios. "It's all about environment. The feel. The look. Everything," Emma added. "We've got to show them that we're not just about their business. We're about…" *Okay, I've run out of steam.*

The truth was, Evan made Emma's insides tingle. She felt herself flush when he stood near to her admiring the room. She hoped no one else noticed. She felt so transparent at that time. This was awkward. His deep voice, his charm, his physique. She had to refocus. "...them," she finished.

Evan nodded as he walked around. He had trusted her with her input. She really wanted to be senior on this account. To move up the ranks. To manage this baby.

Though the others walked in with their hands behind their backs at her little surprise-she made Evan promise earlier not to look or to let anyone else in as she got the boardroom done up—they didn't look as impressed with the décor as Evan. They thought he shouldn't trust a junior staff member as much and go with the simple, professional look and stick to the business side of things. After all, to them, she was still part of the reception staff and a former college student. It was hard for some to shake that initial first impression image of her. She was glad Evan believed in her enough to take charge.

Evan was taking a chance on Emma's idea, and as such, he was sticking by her.

Of course, she had something else in mind, too. But she had to push that to the back of her mind.

The group gathered round the table as they went over their roles in the presentation that would only last ten minutes in itself. Each spoke as they went around the table. Evan leaned back in the chair stroking his chin as he listened in on everyone's input. He looked as if he were pondering in deep thought. He nodded occasionally. He had masterminded many great advertising campaigns, but what Emma admired about him was that he was willing to let someone else or others step up to the plate and spoon out their own delight. He always gave others a chance. Just as he was giving her an opportunity to shine with the wedding campaign.

But he threw a gaze directly at Emma from time to time which made her flush, shift uncomfortably on her seat, and pray to God no one else in the room noticed. Perhaps she was reading into this too much.

The graphic designer put on display the most exquisite looking gowns, wedding cakes, and flowers. Emma swore the whole environment was enough to seduce anyone into the mood for getting hitched. Heck, if she hadn't been burned by an ex-flame in the past, she may even want to give it a go, for real this time.

With an assistant by her side, Ms. Kelsia Endo, the owner of Weddings R U, came into the office with quite a presence. Her head held up extraordinarily high. She was dressed in a long pink coat and a long pink dress with pearls that glowed. Her earrings were bold and as large as her ears. Emma could not help but notice the bling. They sparkled. She tried hard as she reached to shake her hand not to stare, but it was just so in your face.

She wore a large rimmed church-style hat suitable for a queen. The only thing missing was gloves. In her bright pink matching coat and dress, Evan ushered her inside the reception area and gave her a tour. She seemed at first rather stoic. The story was that she was a romantic at heart. Her beloved husband died many years prior and left her with a whole whack of money. Millions. She decided to invest in her own start-up business. Making others' wedding dreams come true. She was also the daughter of some wealthy socialite of African British background.

"Yes, it's beautiful," she commented with her head held up high. She barely looked at Emma. Her only non-verbal assessment was a quick look at Emma's cleavage. Emma swallowed. Great, first impression. She really wanted to win the account despite Ms. Endo's standoffish first impression.

"Mr. Fletcher, your office is impeccable."

"Thanks, I'm glad you like it. And please, call me Evan."

"Very well, Evan."

Emma could tell that Evan was half-waiting for her to say "please, call me Kelsia," but that didn't look like that would be happening any time soon.

When Ms. Endo walked into the boardroom, she froze. Her eyes widened.

Emma swallowed hard. She could tell that Evan did, too. Was this a horrible mistake?

"It is…" Ms. Endo gaped around the room, leaving everyone in suspense. "Exquisite. I've never had an agency go through such effort. It looks like…like the reception I had with dear old Percy before he left to be with the angels. God rest his soul." She clasped her hands to her chest.

Okay, maybe it wasn't such a bad idea after all. As Ms. Endo strolled ahead of them, Evan squeezed Emma's shoulder. Emma felt her insides turn to jelly. She thought her knees would buckle beneath her.

She drew in a deep breath. She hated giving presentations. She would much rather be taking a bath in tar and feathers than to give a speech. But she digressed. She would get on with it. Evan had coached her earlier on deep breathing and visualization during these pitches— stuff she learned in college, of course. He would remind her to try picturing everyone in the boardroom naked— which would make her giddy inside if she dare visualize sexy Evan with no clothes on.

Perhaps it was not such a good idea today, since she would end up blushing or lusting throughout her little spiel.

Evan outlined the storyboard for the TV ad as Ms. Endo helped herself to the refreshments.

Ms. Endo seemed to be enjoying the pastries as much as the presentation. She was already impressed after reading the Fletcher Advertising Company information booklet which Evan and Emma had worked hard in putting together over the past two years. The executive summary, bio, other clients served, their services, vision, and sample of successful ad campaigns graced the cover of the book, and though most of the information was available on the website, many clients preferred a hard copy.

She carefully took a bite out of each freshly baked pastry on her plate and washed them down with a glass of non-alcoholic wine. "What a marvellous touch," she gushed and licked her fingers as her assistant typed notes on her laptop. She gently wiped her hands on a designer napkin and continued to feast her eyes on the presentation.

There was talk of how Weddings R Us provided more than the proverbial picture perfect wedding. They took the stress out of planning a wedding. A one-stop design center. Need help choosing the wedding cake? No problem. Want to know about the latest cake trends? Weddings R Us is there. They have affordable wedding planners on site for the cost of less than a wedding dress. They'll do the counselling, planning, preparation, menu options, venue selection, wedding dress consultation and design, all you need to do is dial 555-weddings-r-us and leave the rest to us. "Less Stress and More Success" was the slogan that was pushed during the meeting.

After her presentation, Ms. Endo gave Emma a blank stare. She then lifted up her hands and clapped. Her assistant and the rest of the team joined. "Wonderful." She nodded her head. "Very impressive, indeed."

Emma let out a deep sigh of relief but tried to stifle it.

Much later, at the end of the day, the team had already cleared out of the boardroom and prepared to leave on time after the overtime they'd been putting in to prepare for the big pitch.

Evan walked in while Emma and Lucinda cleared out the boardroom. He had already pulled down most of the ads on the wall and helped restack some of the chairs.

"You ladies need help?"

"Oh, almost done. Thanks," Emma said cheerfully.

"Well, I have to leave, I've got a dentist appointment." Lucinda looked at her watch. It seemed as if she wanted to stay when she caught a glimpse of Emma and Evan locked briefly in a stare before they uncomfortably diverted their eyes elsewhere.

"Thanks for your help, Lucinda. See you tomorrow." Evan locked off the elevators that opened up directly on to the floor after Lucinda left. He probably wanted to make sure everything would be locked, though Lucinda usually tackled that chore as the receptionist and office manager.

Clearly everyone was pumped by the response at the presentation. It went exceptionally well, to say the least. Ms. Endo winked at Evan as she grabbed his arm to say that she had already made her choice. Expect a call from her office tomorrow. That was good news, indeed. Evan was far more relaxed. He was so thankful for his team. Once all went well and official, he would assign Emma as the main person on the account to work with him.

"I especially loved that added touch with the stats," Evan offered.

"Oh, that's nothing."

"No, that was something." He smiled a deep, dimpled grin. "Ms. Endo loved the figures." And he loved Emma's figure. "You really hit it home, stating that every year there are 2.34 million weddings in the U.S." He paced as he recounted her speech. "People spend on average $60 billion a year not counting the honeymoon. Nice. Then, you showed how Weddings R Us can alleviate the stress and pressure of producing the best while they take care of the rest."

"Feel your best and we'll take care of the rest," Emma continued. They both held up a glass from the boardroom and clinked to cheer.

"Hope we're not being premature." Emma sipped her beverage.

"Whatever the outcome, we put on a great presentation. We should be proud," he said with conviction.

"So, you wanted to ask me something?" Evan's voice was deep, relaxed, and inviting. He had his hands shoved in his pocket as he walked over to Emma. He looked directly into her almond brown eyes. She had the right mix of eye makeup. Not too much, not too little. Just enough to accent her beautiful large, brown eyes. They were so innocent looking.

So bright. Hopeful.

And those lips. God, he loved those full lips. So defined. She had the most naturally beautiful features he'd ever seen on a woman and he loved how she held court with herself. She wasn't arrogant about her good looks. He figured she probably didn't even realize how beautiful she was.

He was turned on by her inner beauty as well as her exterior charm.

Emma swallowed hard. Her heartbeat raced in her chest. She feared he would hear the lub-dub sound pounding from the very core of her being. If she thought she was nervous giving the presentation, what about now?

She had finished clearing the table and held up her folder with her notes to her chest to comfort her. A psychological shield. Or something to stop her hands from quivering.

"Yes, actually, I did have a question to ask." Oh, God, how on earth am I going to do this? If only this was a presentation to a client instead of a proposal to my boss. She sucked in a deep breath.

Evan leaned over by the side table with a salacious grin on his face, arms folded beneath his pecs. Waiting.

God, his dimples are so sexy. So inviting.

He was sweet and smooth as honey, Emma concluded. This didn't make it any easier. She was glad the office was clear. But then a sudden thought struck her. It was just she and Evan in the office complex.

Alone.
Together.

She could hear the sound of the ice machine in the pantry and the muffled roar of the evening rush hour traffic outside the window. And the beat of her own heart.

You can do this, Emma.

What's the worst that could happen?

Um. I could lose my job, my reputation, my world, and my chances of a happily ever after...

Okay, focus, Emma. Think positive. This isn't the end of the world. Or your life.

Now was the time for her to replace her inner-worrier with her inner-warrior. Emma took another deep breath and decided to go along with the truth. Well, the abridged version. What Evan needed to know. About her grandfather. The promise that prematurely spilled out of her mouth, but as she commenced to speak, she could barely meet Evan's eyes. At last, the whole convoluted story came tumbling out. For more dramatic effect, she paced around the boardroom telling her story, especially the finale. The part about her grandfather arranging for them to get married by the end of next week. When she finished, she turned to face Evan.

Her breath stopped.

Evan froze on the spot with his arms still snugly folded across his chest, eyes glazed in shock staring at her. The honey-caramel tanned color of his skin had drained from his face. There wasn't a sign of the earlier friendly, warm expression that he donned moments before. Not a trace of it dressed his face.

Emma wished at that moment the ground would open up and swallow her whole. Or a giant serpent would eat her in one gulp. Or she could melt. Die. She didn't care! Okay, now might be a safe time to panic. Had she just made the most career-ending, friendship-destroying mistake of her life?

6

"You did what?" Evan had heard and seen a lot in his thirty-three years, especially in the corporate climbing world of advertising, but never had he ever encountered anything of this magnitude. He could not believe his ears. They burned. His mouth felt parched all of the sudden. He could feel his blood curdle.

He unfroze from his position and got up from leaning on the side table. He took a deep breath. He did not let his eyes move from Emma's.

Emma parted her lips to say something but immediately clamped her mouth shut tightly again. She realized it was a rhetorical question. Of course, he wouldn't want to hear the repeat of her spiel of lies she weaved that left him at the center.

He paced with his hands shoved in his pocket of his pants. He had already taken off his jacket and loosened his tie after the meeting.

Then, he laughed. His eyes diverted momentarily to the April evening sky; the sun was beginning to set and traffic was lightening as the headlights beamed from the cars driving to their destinations. The town hillside looked gorgeous from the view of his ceiling to floor window in the boardroom. He had to gather his thoughts. He had to choose his words carefully. He shook his head.

This was Emma Wiggins, his prized employee. His secret crush. His partner. His…

Part of him was in shock. But a fraction of him was also quite flattered that she would think of including him in her marital fantasy. Too bad he despised the idea of marriage or anything to do with getting betrothed. Especially on such short notice when he had absolutely no say in the matter. What was she thinking? Had she taken leave of her senses?

He gave much thought before answering. "Now, let me get this straight…" He continued to pace as he looked in her direction, trying to still his temper and keep his cool—as hard as that was. "You told your grandfather that we were engaged?" He could barely usher the words to part from his lips. "And he went ahead and arranged for us to get married next week?"

"Well…yes." Emma could not lie about that part. But she had to go to plan B.

For the first time in his life, Evan was stunned. Speechless. And very little in this world left him in such a state. Not even his father's bizarre behavior from his mental illness.

"Are you for real? Emma, how could you let him think that?"

"Because…Listen, it was never my intention to lie to him. I got caught up in wanting to make him happy. Do the right thing. I honestly thought…" She tried to fight back tears, he could tell. The last thing he wanted to do was make her weep, though what she did was unbelievable.

"I thought I was going to lose him. The doc's still giving him weeks to live. I just wanted to make him happy. To let him think I was at least *getting* married."

Evan stopped cold. He knew what it meant when you love someone and you want to do the right thing. When you feel as if you're going to lose a part of yourself when a loved one departs this world.

He gave it much thought in the time allotted and changed his expression. Emma was pretty much like him. And God, she looked so adorable. So willing to do the right thing even though her actions may be a little off. Her heart was in the right place. He could not fault her there.

Still, she did say the key word "think" she was getting married. Maybe he could grant this dying man a last wish. Heck, last Christmas he faked being Santa Claus for some poor kids in the community just to give them a happy Christmas, even though he didn't believe in Santa Claus any more than he believed in marriage. Why not for his devoted assistant to go along with it?

Just this once.

Why, surely it wouldn't kill him. And with Emma's help, he pretty much landed the Weddings R Us account anyway. He can't be that apposed to the idea of marriage for other people, not if he's representing his client who believed in happily-ever-after-for-two.

Besides, he found Emma to be the most sexy woman he'd ever met and he'd met a lot of beautiful women, but there was something special about her. He knew he would not, could not, ever get married, but why not pretend? It may be the closest he ever got to walking down the aisle with a beautiful bride. If only he could have a not-so-pretend honeymoon with Emma, too. But that would be too much to push right now.

"Fine," he finally uttered. "I'll go along with it for next week. We'll pretend to get married."

Emma's heart must have skipped, jumped, and leapt simultaneously. It's a wonder she did not have a heart attack. She could not believe her ears. "You will? Um…thank you so much, Evan. I really do appreciate this." She was flabbergasted he'd agreed to it, considering his stand on marriage.

Wait a minute, did he just say pretend? Uh-oh! Well, I guess I'll have to work on that for next week. At least he'll go along with it for now. That's at least a little headway.

Emma had just finished a long day and needed to go home. Just then, a phone call buzzed in on Evan's BlackBerry.

"Hey, you!" He seemed to be speaking to a woman. "Right, B. Pick you up at eight."

Oh, dear. Pick you up at eight? That doesn't sound good.

"Oh, sorry. Didn't mean to keep you from your date," Emma gushed.

"It's not exactly a date."

Emma tried to hide her relief and sighed inside her mind. Then another thought hit her. If it's not exactly a date, then what is it? Now that they were sort of pretending to get married next week, she really needed him not to be dating other women. How was this going to work out? Emma really needed to tell him that he really had to go along with it—all the way. Then they could get an annulment after. She bit down on her lower lip. She knew she would be damned forever for lying. But she really didn't want to take real vows. Since the chaplain at the hospital would be involved, she would sort of have to take vows. How much should she tell Evan? So far, he thinks they are faking it. Emma took another swig of the non-alcoholic wine.

Faking it was definitely not going to be easy.

7

Evan rolled over in his king size bed. Emma was beside him, naked under the covers. A grin as wide as the Mercy Springs Lake sprawled across his face. He could not believe what transpired last night. The passion, the lovemaking…. The loud beeping sound of the alarm caused him to flinch. Annoyed, he reached over and hit the snooze button. Talk about bad timing. When he leaned over to give his assistant a good morning squeeze, she was gone.

"Emma?"

There was absolutely no sign of her or that she'd even been at his cosy condominium last night. He flipped onto his back with his hands behind his head, grinned, and shook his head.

It was only in his dream.

He could not believe he dreamed of making passionate love to Emma last night. It was as real as it seemed, and he thought she'd stayed the night. Why was he thinking of her so much? He really needed to get a life. She was his assistant, nothing more.

Then a stunning thought struck him upside his head. His heart sank.

Did I promise Emma I'd pretend to marry her next week?

He could not believe it. Now, in hindsight, it all seemed so…damn crazy.

He sprung out of bed and stretched as he headed for his ensuite bathroom with the granite top counters and marbled floor.

Maybe that whole getting married next week gig was nothing more than a crazy dream as well. Maybe he'd imagined the whole damn thing. The idea sounded as crazy as he felt. Why or how could she even propose such a thing? He was her boss for heaven's sake.

When he gazed at his image in the bathroom mirror—looking at the man he'd become, he thought to himself how much he'd wish the part about Emma spending the night with him wasn't simply some fantasy. Heck, it wasn't just about a one-night stand either.

Was he missing something in his life?

Up to this point, it hadn't really dawned on him. He'd just made a decision to live the life of a carefree bachelor. His entire life. He didn't want to be chained down or imprisoned in the institution called marriage. His mind flicked back to the incident with his father. God, he didn't want to end up in pieces over a woman. That damn "Fletcher Curse!" He swore the words out of his mouth while brushing his teeth with his battery operated toothbrush and spat out the toothpaste with vengeance as if spewing his thoughts of marriage out into the sink, hoping the idea of marital commitment would slither down the drain pipe and never surface again.

Evan got washed up, dressed for an early morning workout at the gym before work, then headed out the door with his car keys, gym bag, and briefcase.

Emma rushed into the hospital as quickly as she could. She needed to see her grandfather before heading to work. She knew her time with him was limited. The doctors and nurses had told her that every day was different.

He could be responsive and seem okay one day, only to end up tentative and weak the next. Unfortunately, that was the nature of his illness. It was hard to say what kind of day he would have.

Emma shivered inside at the thought of losing him, forever. She remembered the time she had visited not so long ago when he seemed as stiff as a slab of wood. Lifeless. His meal trays untouched. She flinched at the idea of him alone with no visitors when…the worst should happen. She wanted to hold his hand, to be with him every chance she got. She would never, could never, forgive herself if she started or ended her day without gracing his day with a friendly, warm visit.

She would often visit on her way to work to make sure he was eating his breakfast. Emma had already picked up two fresh baked biscuits and muffins for them to devour while she visited him briefly. The aroma of the biscuits made her mouth water, though she resisted the desire to break off some and eat before she got there. She held her own coffee in one hand. Her grandfather didn't care too much for it. When he was up to it, he'd drink juice or plain water.

Sometimes the nursing staff didn't have time to sit and make sure he ate everything on the plate. They told her that at the stage in his illness, they wouldn't be forcing him to eat. Comfort was their main concern for him. As long as he was hydrated and not suffering, they assured her.

Sometimes the patients experienced a sharp decrease in appetite, something about part of the dying process. She flinched at the whole idea. Still, Emma wanted to do whatever she could. It was more for her than anything else, she guiltily admitted. She wouldn't know what to expect each morning she did visit her beloved Gramps.

She briefly glanced down at her watch, it was a little before seven o'clock in the morning. She smiled at the security guard as she walked into the elevator. He nodded in return.

"Keep that beautiful smile," he said as he waved to her.

"Thanks," she responded with a flush as she boarded the elevator going up to the seventh floor long-term and palliative care unit.

Mr. H happened to be sitting in his wheelchair in the elevator with a cup of coffee from Starbucks. He obviously had been down to the lower level food court at the hospital. When she hopped on from the main floor he smiled to her.

"You know, it's not everyone who waves and smiles at the security guard or the man sweeping the street. That old man raised you well, didn't he?" he chuckled.

"Oh, Mr. H!" Emma blushed. She really had to get used to accepting a compliment graciously, that was something she really didn't do to well. She always fobbed it off or downplayed her actions. "It's no big deal. Everyone deserves a nice hello. Every job's important. So is everybody."

Mr. H smiled and eyed her with his own sense of pride as he tilted his head.

"So, how is your daughter and new son-in-law? Have they left on their honeymoon yet?" Emma asked.

"Oh, yes. They're leaving for Jamaica today. Sandals resort, I believe." He glowed when he spoke of them. The wedding was only two days ago, but it seemed so fresh as it if just happened that instant.

"Marriage is a beautiful thing, isn't it?" He took a sip of his coffee, and without missing a beat, he turned his attention back to Emma. "So, where are you and your groom going on your honeymoon?"

Emma almost choked on her coffee. She hadn't been prepared for that. Though it was silly really. That should be at the forefront of her mind. She almost forgot that she was getting married next week and that Mr. H would, of course, be one of her guests.

"Um. Well, we hadn't really thought about that yet. We decided to take it one step at a time. You know, this whole short notice business."

Which was partly true, though guilt was a poor appetizer, wasn't it? Suddenly, Emma didn't feel too much like eating, and swallowing coffee seemed like an arduous chore at that point. She could taste the bitterness of deceit. The aftertaste was nothing to be admired. Guilt tore at her. Suddenly, she didn't feel so wonderful. Why did she lie? How could she keep up this charade? And the whole fake business. She had to clarify with Evan that this was for real. A real chaplain from the hospital would be performing the honors. There would be real guests. Real flowers. Real vows. Real…heartbreak if this didn't go through as planned. She could barely look Mr. H in the eyes after that. She hoped, prayed he wouldn't see the look of guilt and deceit spread across her face.

Suddenly, the seventh floor couldn't come soon enough. It seemed forever to reach that level. When the ding sound of the elevator alerted them to the appropriate floor, relief that she no longer had to continue the conversation washed over her. She smiled and waved to Mr. H as he wheeled himself by pushing his feet along the ground towards the lounge. He had firmly declined when she offered to wheel him to his room or to where wherever it was he wanted to go. He felt strong today and independence was something he was not about to give up any time soon. When Emma saw that he was okay, she walked down the hospital unit's long corridor, noticing the nurses were all in the report room for shift change. The unit smelled of fresh pine. The floors had apparently been recently polished. She saw a few hospital support staff in scrubs cleaning up. Sometimes it was difficult to tell who was who. Not all the nurses on that unit had their stethoscopes slung over their necks and some of the support staff wore scrubs. She sort of missed the earlier days when nurses wore white. It was obvious who was who when she needed assistance. Once, when she had visited her grandfather, when he started to vomit, she erroneously asked a support staff to get something to make him stop and asked what meds he ingested that day. Her scattered thoughts vanished when she at last reached the room number where her grandfather was situated.

Horror struck her when she arrived at his room. She dropped her drink on the floor and rushed in.

Evan leaned back in his executive chair in his office peering out the window.

He enjoyed soaking up the beautiful view from his corner office window overlooking one of Texas's beautiful lakes. The small town of Mercy Springs had it good where location was concerned. The blueness of the water seemed to glisten in the early spring morn. It was seven o'clock in the morning. Evan loved to get an early start to the day before anyone reached the office. This gave him a chance to clear his mind and prepare for the day ahead.

He already had an early run to get his cardio done for the day and showered in the executive showers in the gym on the ground floor of the facilities. He deliberately chose the newly built glass building with a plush restaurant, health club, and other offices on its premises for its perks.

It was all about convenience. He loved the place. In a funny way, work had always been his sanctuary, his escape from what, well, he didn't know. All he knew was that with the frustration and disappointment he'd dealt with, it was the one place where, oddly enough, he felt he had more control. No doubt about it, he excelled at what he did and his office wall was decorated with many prestigious ad industry awards he'd won alongside his agency.

He leaned forward in his chair and took another swig of his latte before immersing himself in a brochure he'd been working on for another client. Though he felt, actually almost knew, in his gut that he'd won the Weddings R Us account, he wasn't going to break out the bubbly just yet, and he was definitely not going to put his other accounts and contracts in second gear. Every client would receive the same star treatment.

As he analysed the ad for a women's magazine, he could not help but flicker his thoughts back to Emma. What was going through his mind? He could not believe the events that unfolded last night. The promise he'd made to Emma. Had it been a spur of the moment decision affected by his victory performance at the new client pitch? Or was it something else? No question about it. Fascination with Emma gripped him and wouldn't untether him..

He was in love with her. He couldn't explain it. He thought he should be as far away from her as possible. But now he was going to be walking down the aisle, albeit improvised in a hospital ward, with her.

Next week!

Had he gone stark mad? Or madly in love that he'd do anything, seize any opportunity to play married with her. Heck, it was better than the real thing. Was this what love did to a person? Numb a person's reserve of common sense?

Only time would tell.

Emma rushed over to her grandfather in his hospital room and kneeled down to his side. She cast her handbag on the floor out of the way. He sat crouched low at his bedside, his spectacles on the ground. "Gramps! Are you alright?"

At first, her grandfather seemed a little disoriented. He seemed unharmed. His glazed, startled look caused Emma's heart to palpitate until he finally recognised her and a grin perched on his lips. "Oh, yes. Fine, pumpkin. How are you doing?" He let out a little nervous chuckle. Or was that embarrassment?

Emma allowed a deep sigh of relief to escape. "Gramps, did you fall?" she asked, panic rising again in her chest. She did not wait for him to answer but held him with one hand while she reached over with the other to push the nurse call bell cord hanging off the bed rail. She dared not leave him unattended until she knew he was fine.

"Oh. No, no, dear. You see, I just wanted to grab that piece of paper on the counter over there. It has all the numbers on it."

"The numbers? What numbers, Gramps?" She began to wonder if he were getting confused.

"The numbers," he sighed heavily. "You know, for the wedding list. I still have more people to invite. To call. We only have next week, you know."

Emma gulped. Her eyes darted to the newly cleaned hospital floor. The weight of guilt sure made for heavy eyelids. "Right. Of course." This was real, wasn't it? She really did have to go through with this. Oh, what had she done?

"Yes, can I help you? Oh, no!" The nurse rushed to Mr. Wiggins's side. "Mr. Wiggins, are you alright? What happened?" The nurse then turned to Emma.

After Emma explained what had transpired—or what she did or did not see, the nurse called for assistance.

The doctor also came in. They spoke to her grandfather and assessed him for evidence of a fall. His vitals were taken and recorded and he was deemed stable for his condition. The nurse spoke of entering in an incident report. They seemed satisfied with his explanation that he got weak when he got up and simply sat down on the floor, too powerless to climb back into bed. The custodian also came to clean up the coffee spill from Emma's own incident when she first arrived on the scene.

After they ate and laughed at a few of her grandfather's jokes, Emma was relieved that the episode wasn't serious. She glanced at her watch and realised that time fleeted too quickly. She called the office and told Lucinda to pass on the message that she'd be a little late coming in since she was held up at the hospital. Work was vital. Crucial. Everything to her. But more and more she realised how important her grandfather was and how she longed for him to be happy during his final days.

She really wanted to pull off this wedding thing, since it was the last thing she could do. She only wished, longed for it to be the real deal. But maybe, that was asking too much. Of course it was, she corrected herself. Who asks their boss to marry them out of the blue?

It was ten after nine o'clock when Emma finally made it into the office.

She knew or at least hoped Evan wouldn't mind. It wasn't as if she were slacking off, after all. She'd put in a whole lot of overtime for no extra pay on her client work in addition to working on the big pitch for Weddings R Us.

When she arrived at reception, her heart almost stopped.

Evan stood there in his suit, an angry look plastered over his face with his hands crossed over his chest. Lucinda, the receptionist, the graphic designer, and copywriter all had serious looks on their faces. More like stony, icy looks targeted at her.

Had she done something wrong? What was with everyone? She really didn't need this. She'd already had one scare this morning. No, another one could not be on tap for the day.

Her heart thumped hard and loud in her chest, she was sure they could auscultate the beats from where they stood.

She swallowed with more animation than necessary, racking her brain for what could have caused her to be the recipient of everyone's displeasure this morning.

She approached cautiously as she came through the glass double door to the reception area where everyone stood, apparently waiting for her.

"Is everything okay?" she asked slowly, her eyebrows wrinkled, a puzzled look spread on her face. She gaped around at everyone's faces for perhaps support, answers, friendliness. Anything? Nothing.

Evan unclenched his arms, shoved his hands in his pocket, and held his chin up. "Actually, Emma…" he paused then tilted his head back down to stare directly into her eyes with an unreadable expression dressing his face.

Then slowly, the look of gravity, or was that disgust, seemed to fade from his face and dissolved into a pleasant…grin?

"Congratulations. You've done it! You—well, all of us, but especially your input into yesterday's boardroom session, landed the Weddings R Us account."

Everyone, including Emma and Evan, let out a celebratory cheer and relaxed their stoic expressions. They all went over to hug her.

"What? I don't understand…"

"Well, Ms. Endo said it was the nice touch with the boardroom theme that clinched the deal. She said it was a close race. Neck in neck with the other ad agency. She loved us. Especially what we—you did-with the wedding theme, going the extra mile." Evan walked over and hugged her shoulder. "Too early for champagne, but we'll be having lunch at Brenna's Restaurant to celebrate. Hope you didn't bring lunch today."

"Well, actually, no, I didn't."

"Good. We also need to chat later about you working senior on the account. Just as we discussed. The team is all for it. We can talk more later."

"Um. Sure." Emma felt the heat rise in her cheeks.

She was gobsmacked. She didn't know how to react. She was stunned. Exhilarated, but stunned nevertheless. That Evan, she could pinch him. He really had her all worked up. She had to hand it to him, he really had her fooled. They *all* did.

Much later, Evan met with Emma in his office and they went over her taking on a bigger role with Weddings R Us. The sky outside was a blinding blue. Everything seemed so clear. Emma could feel the heat from the window from the beaming sunlight. Talk about a perfect spring day. The blueness of the lake in the backdrop was clearly visible through the window behind Evan as he sat leaned back in his chair while he spoke with her. He seemed so dreamy. He had on a shirt and tie since he was meeting with another client later in the day. The muscular physique was hard not to notice through his shirt sleeves. He certainly had biceps to die for. She wondered what it would be like to bury herself in his arms. Locked in a passionate embrace. She visualised him underneath his shirt. Without a shirt. Without anything on.

Okay, stop it, Emma. Focus on work.

She had to remind herself that he was still her employer—though next week, he would end up her pretend groom.

They had a conference call with the client to go over more details on the launch and the ad campaign and spoke about travelling to New York to begin work on the shoot.

Emma's heart raced at the thought of travelling to New York with Evan. Alone. Just the two of them. She wondered if they would have a moment to discuss their impending wedding next week, speaking of Weddings R Us. She couldn't help but think of the irony with getting married and launching a wedding account with a major client.

"Speaking of weddings," Evan paused as he leaned back in his chair, a cute dimpled grin perched on his face. His striking facial features made Emma melt. He was gorgeous in every sense of the word. His rich, dark skin tone and dark, mysterious features, chiselled cheek bones, and deep, rich voice made her insides flutter. Thousands of tiny butterflies sprung wild in her belly. She tried to resist salivating over the man. God, she wished she were going to be his bride, for real.

"Yes?"

"Seems like quite a dramatic irony. The "Weddings" account, then you spring this wedding thing on me." He smiled and Emma thought she saw a salacious look in his eyes. Seductive. Or was that wishing thinking?

"Funny, I was thinking the same thing. What a coincidence." She gave a nervous chuckle. Okay, now was the time to tell him about the slight alteration in their upcoming "fake" wedding—which may not be so fake after all.

He flipped through his organiser on his desk. "What date was that wedding, again?" He furrowed his brow.

"Oh, my grandfather planned it for next Friday." She felt sweat moisten her silk blouse and wondered if her top would cling to her skin.

He paused and leaned back, his hand touching his chin in thought. Pondering. Deciphering what to do next.

"Does that interfere with our trip to New York?" She secretly wished the answer would be no.

"Oh, no, we'll be back by then." When he spoke the words, Emma expunged a sigh of relief. She hadn't realised she actually stopped breathing while she anticipated his answer.

"In fact—"

A knock on the door interrupted his sentence. It was Lucinda. Does she not believe in forwarding a call via telecommunication? Getting up from reception and walking over to Evan's office seemed to be one of her favourite pastimes. Emma recalled when she worked at reception, she was never to leave her desk, unless it was for a bathroom break or another urgent matter. Couriers gladly came over for her to sign parcels. There was no need really. Except for the odd ergonomic stretch, of course.

Though it is an open space concept, Emma always thought if a visitor or client waltzes in, it would be ideal to have the receptionist, well, at the reception desk.

The office had a door chime and bell at the glass reception table. The area was quite plush with tall windows from ceiling to floor. When you walked in, you were treated to a breathtaking view of the outside, the lake, the busy roads, the city, the landscape. Then, of course, the reception desk appeared before you.

Evan really picked an awesome, inspiring concept when he found the building, Emma had to credit him. The artsy, futuristic looking loft gave it a nice touch, too.

"Sorry to trouble you, Evan, but Bianca's on line one." Lucinda smiled at Evan and waited for him to respond.

"Thank you, Lucinda. I'll take the call." He gestured to Emma to wait while he picked up the receiver. The smile widened on Lucinda's face as she walked off. The smile vanished on Emma's as Evan punched line one.

Bianca? Again?

Emma tried hard not to listen to the conversation but not as much as she suppressed the urge to squirm in her seat. She was on edge now. But not as much as Evan, apparently. She noticed a drastic change in his body language. He leaned forward on the desk and his face looked flushed. He listened most of the time. Nodding in thought. Answering occasionally.

What was going on between them? Still, she tried to rationalise that it was none of her business. Though it sort of bothered her that this woman, his ex-girlfriend, had the sort of priority-interrupt-any-meeting-when-she-calls treatment. Emma embarrassingly recognised the feelings she experienced whenever Bianca phoned and interrupted anything at the office to speak with Evan.

Jealousy.

When Evan got off the phone call, he seemed preoccupied in his thoughts.

"Sorry about that. Personal business."

"Sure. No probs." Emma's smile seemed forced, Evan even noticed. Was she jealous? Did she think there was something going on between him and Bianca? Or something rekindling with Bianca? Not a chance. He chuckled and was about to address her body language and non-verbal concerns when another call came in. He realised Lucinda put it through. He picked it up.

"Uh-huh. Yep. Great. Perfect." He hung up.

"Everything's all set for our New York trip. You have your travel docs, right?"

"Oh, of course," Emma responded with an air of distraction.

"Okay, so we'll be heading out tomorrow—if that's okay? Client wants to see us a.s.a.p."

"Sure. I'm game."

He noticed her octave higher than usual falsetto voice. She was eager to please but he sensed a hint of hesitation, or was that anxiety? Maybe he should explain about the whole Bianca thing so that she didn't get any ideas.

For some reason, he felt the need to explain himself to her. It wasn't as if they were really getting married.

What was he going crazy about? It was only a pretence.

But he felt, oddly, obligated to be up front with Emma about everything. That's the old Fletcher thing again, wasn't it? Devoted to a fault. And for what? To have your heart taken for granted, trampled on, then left for nothing?

He tried not to think of his father at the moment. And what the other Fletcher men in his family had gone through, not to mention his own personal heartbreak, but still, whenever a woman came into the picture, it was hard not to think of what could happen. He certainly did have a weakness alright.

Pretty women.

Smart, beautiful, kind-hearted, got-it-together women. Just like Emma.

Only Emma.

What is wrong with me? Evan asked for the fifty-sixth time.

Evan could tell this was a lot for Emma. Account coordinator one day. High flying ad exec the next. Still, he believed in her and it wasn't as if she'd be travelling alone. She looked adorable in her pink silk top. He tried hard not to gape at her breasts. The shape of her nipples became visible through her blouse. God, he was beginning to get turned on. He had to shift his focus on something else. Oh, yeah, the client. Bianca. His father. The wedding next week. Okay, maybe not the wedding next week or the honeymoon he wished they could have following next week's farcical nuptials.

He tried to think of what else he was about to say to her before his tempting interruption. Heck, before her nipples made a surprise appearance. But he could think of nothing else except how much he wanted to see her naked. Alone with him. And how much he wished he could just—

"Evan?"

"Yes?" He jolted upright.

He felt blood rush to the areas it shouldn't right now. He knew for damn sure he was blushing. He straightened up his composure. He dared not stand up right now—he may not be the only thing standing up.

He really didn't want to frighten Emma away. They were, after all, going to New York together. A whole lot of stuff can happen in a city known for spontaneous actions and hot romance like New York. Heck, it was worse than Vegas!

For the next hour, the spoke about last minute details regarding travel arrangements. They would meet at the office then head out to the airport first thing in the morning. He asked how her grandfather was doing. She explained and he was relieved that everything was okay. Emma knew very little about his father's condition except that he wasn't doing so well. She also asked Evan how his dad was doing.

"Oh, he's good, thanks for asking." A troubled expression was evident on his face. "Well, much better now, anyway," he corrected.

"Oh?"

Evan explained a little to Emma, not too much—he felt some things needed to be private for now.

He really wasn't one to lay out his personal life or that of his father to his employees or coworkers, as he would often refer to them. He just mentioned that his father had some trouble with the home care nurse, so he'd hired someone he was familiar with, someone he knew his father trusted and liked. His friend, Bianca. He noticed a slight shift in Emma's stiff body language as he explained Bianca's role and why it was crucial he took calls from her immediately in case there was a critical situation with his father.

He couldn't remember if he had told Emma they were an item at one point and time. He'd had quite a few dates coming into the office to meet him for dinner after work or such. Emma was discreet about it all, especially when she worked at reception. Not that there was anything serious between him and Bianca. But she was a community nurse after all, and a nurse who had experience working with mentally ill patients.

His father had met Bianca on a few occasions and took a strong liking to her personality. Her wit, her charm, her no-nonsense caring demeanour.

Evan thought she would be perfect. And so far, minor glitches aside, the arrangement seemed to be working much better than the other home care staff. This took a load off his mind so that he could focus on work once again.

He didn't have to worry about Bianca's feelings for him. She'd moved on a long time ago. In fact, she was now living with someone who made her visibly happy. Evan was glad for that. He knew he could not have given her the commitment she craved. Still, his past feelings for Bianca were nothing compared to the strong, hard-to-explain, cosmic-attraction he had with Emma.

8

Later that night, Emma sat on her balcony with her BlackBerry in her hand and a glass of wine in the other, her heart pounding hard and fast.

She sucked in a deep breath before pressing down on the number one key to retrieve her voicemail. She knew she couldn't keep putting this off forever. She had to face the melody and hoped the conversation she would later have with her mother would not throw her off key.

"You have one new message. First message," the disembodied woman's voice announced on the voicemail retrieval system.

"Hi, darling, it's your mother. I just heard from your grandfather about your wedding. I didn't even know you were engaged. Guess we haven't spoken in a while. Still, I wished you'd have called me, dear. Anyway, give me a call when you get this message. We'll try to make it in for next week. No promises though. This is such short notice. Well, by for now." Beep.

The pre-recorded voice returned after Emma listened to her mother's message. "To listen to this message again, press four. To save this message, press nine. To erase this message, press seven."

She really didn't want to hear the message again. The guilt was way too much. What could she say to her mother? How much longer could she keep up this deceit, this charade? One thing's for sure, she'd sworn to never tell a lie again—and she'd come to the realisation, there's no such thing as a "little" white lie. It's either an untruth or it isn't. Plain and simple.

Emma had a lot of thoughts sprinting through her mind at that moment, the trip to New York, facing Evan again, the new account, her own pretend, fairy tale, beautiful wedding, oh, stop it Emma! The wedding was a sham! And now she had to keep up the charade and tell her mother a not-so-little, off-white lie.

She switched phones and got her cordless house phone, thankful she had a good long distance plan for North America and dialled the long distance number to Toronto, Canada. She gazed up at the sky. Daylight savings ended recently and she was glad it was still light outside. The cool evening breeze blew gently on the balcony. She sat back in her Wal-Mart purchased patio chair and placed her glass on the matching table. She worked hard and tried to make her little home as cosy and comfortable as possible. Especially for use after a long day at work. She had a pretty good view of the landscape. Her building overlooked a park, some new homes in the development, the quiet street, and she could see in the distance the hills and trees farther south. She looked up at the blue sky with the streak of reddish sunset peeking through.

The view was tranquil. Stunning. Breathtaking. Because it was a more subdued part of town, she enjoyed the reduction of noisy traffic and choking pollution. She could just hear distant laughter of children in the background. Stillness. The air smelled, oddly, clean and clear. She enjoyed these moments to sit and peer out from the balcony. She was grateful for the view she had from her floor.

Secretly, she dreamed of living in an expensive, upscale condominium complex with a state-of-the-art gym facility, tennis court, indoor swimming pool and sauna, gated security, concierge desk, close to stores and other conveniences, and a new neighbourhood. Still, she was genuinely grateful for what she had. What was that old saying, "Don't be sad for what you don't have, be glad for what you *do* have." And that other saying, "Gratitude leads to abundance." She couldn't remember where she'd read it, probably from one of her self-help New Age books that she shelved on her antique oak bookshelf in her living room along with her psych text books.

She was quite content with her slow steady progress in creating a life for herself. She had a job she loved. Her colleagues, especially her boss, loved her. For her work that is. And what other industry do you get to have scrumptious business lunches paid for every other week? Heck, more than that. Earlier they had an awesome celebratory lunch at Brenna's Restaurant and Jazz Club. They had lunch hour music and dining on the patio which was opened at the restaurant since the good southern weather allowed it. It was just perfect. In fact, she couldn't get the look of Evan out of her mind. He seemed to be glancing in her direction every now and then, an almost lustful look to her.

She felt his eyes on her most of the time. Though, she was laughing and talking with the group as they celebrated. They selected the Tex Mex cuisine, which was delicious. Not as tasty as Evan, she thought. She really wished she could just-

"Hello?" Her mother's voice startled her back to reality as the phone was answered. Emma almost forgot she had dialled her mother since the phone had rung so long. Her mother wasn't one for subscribing to voicemail.

Okay, this is it. She sucked in a deep breath. "Hey, Mom. How's it going?"

"Emma. Well, well, well, stranger. Nice of you to call your mom. Almost forgotten what you sound like."

Emma bit down on her lip, her long, soft, curly black hair blowing in her face. She grabbed her free hand to swipe her hair over to her other shoulder. It had been quite a long time since she'd spoken to her mother. They grew quite distant over the years, though she would always make it a point to call on holidays and on her mother's birthday and other occasions. But still, she wished she'd have more time. She had planned to visit her mother in Toronto many times. Maybe she could make a go for it sometime later in the year. She'd heard countless wonderful things about Toronto, the clean streets, the attractions, the friendly people, the Royal Ontario Museum, the Art Gallery of Ontario, and take in the sights at Harborfront. Still, she'd save that for later.

"So how's the weather in Toronto, Mom?"

"Oh, fine, dear. Probably not as hot as Texas at this time of the year." Her mother didn't waste any time with small talk to Emma's chagrin. "So what's this about you getting married next week?"

Okay, here goes.

"Mom, I'm sorry I didn't get to tell you this before—"

"I mean, I didn't even know you were serious with anyone," her mother interrupted.

Emma felt that familiar guilt tinge in the pit of her stomach. Still, she wasn't exactly lying about spending time with Evan. Truth be told, he was the only man she'd spend evenings with—working, that was anyway. She'd worked very closely with him on quite a lot of projects. Had business lunches with him—and the team-while discussing planning strategies for major ad campaigns they were engrossed with.

"What is he like? What does he do for a living? What about his parents?" Her mother was good for spewing a string of questions in a row when she was anxious to solicit information, not giving the person a chance to answer, of course.

Emma answered as much as she could, as truthfully as she could without giving herself away, hating herself every second she misled her mother. But trying to justify by at least thinking that it was all for a good cause. Her grandfather had only weeks to live. She wanted to at least make the last days good, happy, comforting, for the man who practically raised her along with her grandmother after her own father passed away. How bad could that be? Maybe she won't have to spend the rest of her life in regret-hell or damnation if she could help it. If she could somehow make it all okay.

Later that evening, Emma spent the night tossing and turning in bed. She tried hard to get some sort of a good night sleep. But as her grandfather once told her, there's no comfier pillow than a clear conscience. Did she have one or what? Would her conscience ever be clear again.?

She got up and turned on her bedside lamp. It was two o'clock in the morning. She clasped her hand to her forehead. She really needed to get her REM sleep or she was going to look like hell. Not only that, but she'd likely have the mental acuity of a cotton ball at the office. What was bothering her? Being alone with Evan—especially given the new circumstances with the impending wedding nuptials next week.

She sprung up out of bed and powered on her plasma TV but there were only infomercials on most of the stations and reruns of old sitcoms. She couldn't focus on anything right now. The apartment was pretty much quiet, and dark. The sound of the fridge was the only thing she could hear. That and her conscience.

She made herself a cup of camomile tea then went back to her bed. She picked up a riveting mystery novel to see if she could lose herself in a good story to take her mind off her situation before settling to bed.

No headway.

It was useless; her eyes studied the words on the page but nothing was being processed. She glazed over the story. Literally. After finishing the last drop of tea, she went over to her overnight luggage to ensure she had everything all packed and ready. Her notes, her passport. Evan already had the electronic tickets and hotel reservation. God, she hoped to share the same room with him. But enough fantasizing about Evan. He may not want to have anything to do with her when she springs it on him that they are getting married for real next week. The thought had occurred to her and made her queasy to her stomach. She really didn't want to ruin what she could have and her future in advertising with Evan all in one sweep. Still, she had to think positive.

Speaking of which, she grabbed a copy of one of her daily meditation books to read a passage. She read a quote: Your life is whatever you focus on.

Okay.

And another passage: According to the law of attraction, whatever we choose to dwell on we pull into our lives like a magnetic draw. Make sure you focus on what you really want in life, what will be beneficial to you—not what you don't want.

Another passage caught her eye: Practice eradicating thoughts from your mind that distress you.

Yep, easier said than done.

She continued to read: Then replenish with thoughts that promote feelings of happiness. Much like art, any skill can be mastered through dedication and practice.

Okay, that was helpful, she mused. Maybe, she should quit worrying about stuff she has no control over—anymore. Okay, she should have just told Gramps the truth, but it was done now. There was no way to un-ring this bell. The words escaped her lips before she could haul them back—now she just had to play the cards she pulled from the pack and do so the best she could.

After consulting with her travel checklist—something she swears by since she'd been known to leave things behind before—she fluffed up her pillow and slinked back under the duvet covers to finish, or begin might have been a more apt word choice, her few hours of sound sleep. She was determined to partake of a restful slumber. She was going to make this work, even if it killed her.

The following morning, Emma woke up bright and early. The birds were chirping on the balcony. She could hear them outside her window. She jumped up when the alarm sounded, grateful to at least have managed four hours of solid sleep.

She hopped into the shower and got ready for the day. She pulled on a light green cardigan and matching t-shirt underneath and completed the outfit with a beaded necklace and earrings. Comfortable black bootleg pants with a bit of lycra for comfort which hugged her hips and soft leather shoes for her travel were the final touches. Her hair was pinned up above her head and flowed softly onto her shoulders and highlighted her high cheek bones. She grabbed her keys, purse, and luggage and headed for the door to go down to the lobby. She had pre-booked a cab for this morning to take her to the office where she'd meet up with Evan.

When she arrived at the office, she couldn't believe the sight of Evan talking to Lucinda at the reception desk. He turned around when she walked up to them with her black hand luggage on wheels as she tugged it behind her on the hardwood floor.

Evan could have stopped her heart cold with his gorgeous looks.

He often worked out early in the morning. So dedicated to physical fitness. She noticed his naturally wavy, black hair was slicked back. Wet. Sexy. He probably just had a shower after his workout.

She got near enough to him to catch a sensual whiff of his spicy aftershave. The scent tantalised her nostrils. He stood erect, ripping muscles and dark, caramel skin tone, so smooth she was tempted to run her fingers up and down his arms. He wore a t-shirt that showcased his muscular biceps.

The man was ripped, no doubt about that.

She tried to dart her eyes away towards the view out of the glass windows as the sun shined through the reception area. He certainly was blessed with not just his sweet southern charm and talent, but a good physique as well.

She was sure her mouth had fallen open and immediately snapped it shut. She must have appeared to be salivating. Lucinda was shuffling papers in the background at the reception desk while she glanced her way in a discreet way.

Evan paused momentarily when he saw Emma walking through the glass double door of Fletcher Advertising.

She looked stunning.

So simple, yet elegant.

Beautiful.

He still couldn't get those nipples he eyed yesterday out of his mind. But he had to. He must! It was a professional thing to do. Her black pants looked casual, yet elegant, and really showed off her curvaceous form. She had curves in all the right places. She was a perfect figure eight. Heavy on top. Nice rounded thighs and a tiny waist. He didn't know how he was going to keep his mind on business during the next two days—in the Big Apple of all places. The city that never sleeps. He didn't think he would be sleeping much either.

"So, you have everything?" He approached her to help with her luggage.

"Yep, all set."

The sweet, distinctive scent of her perfume drove his testosterone levels up higher than he cared for right now. He had to divert his thoughts onto something else. Other than the stunning, intellectual, kind-hearted beauty before him.

He noticed in his peripheral vision that Lucinda at reception was gawking at them. He hoped whatever he was feeling inside would not be revealed in his expression. He hated that he blushed. Sometimes, he felt hot inside, though the loft was quite cool and comfortable.

He clapped his hands together. "Good, let's get going. My things are in the car."

"The car?" Emma repeated bewildered.

"Yes, I'll be driving and parking at the airport. I think it would be easier, we're just going for two days."

Emma swallowed. She smiled sheepishly. They'd be alone without a driver or third person as they drove half hour to the city airport. Okay, she could do this. Was that a good time to spring the news on him about *really* getting married? She'd have to play it by ear.

9

"You really love her, don't you?" The hospital chaplain sat on a chair at the bedside of Mr. Wiggins. She smiled as she tilted her head. She leaned forward and held his hand as he sat up in the bed.

"Yes. Yes, I really do. She's such a sweetheart. She's a good girl, you know. She really takes care of me." Mr Wiggins smiled as he looked down with mist in his eyes. He fiddled with the bed linen then looked away to stare out the window. The sky was blue. There was nothing but greenery on the hospital grounds outside. His window faced a scenic area of the hospital at the long-term and palliative care wing. His lips began to quiver.

"Is everything alright?" The chaplain, a woman in her mid-fifties with blond, straight hair and the bluest eyes he'd ever seen, squeezed his hand tighter with concern. "You seem upset."

"Oh, it's nothing. I get like this sometimes, you know. I really will miss her. You know, when I'm gone."

"I think she'll miss you, too. Probably more. Life is always hardest for those left behind." The chaplain's voice was low, calming, and soothing. Mr. Wiggins appreciated her nonjudgmental demeanour, especially when he goofed up and said silly things. Of course, Emma would be the one to miss him. What would he know? He'd be dead and gone.

He appreciated the chaplain visiting him every now and again. She often made her rounds to the patients or long-term care residents. He was especially fretting that Emma was heading for New York for a couple of days. Something he knew she hesitated to do knowing full well that his condition—which flipped back and forth on a regular basis—could turn suddenly.

Still, he encouraged Emma to go to New York. He assured her he'd hold on till she got back, he teased her earlier. He understood that she would not be able to see him early this morning as she often did before work since she had to meet her boss—her fiancé—at the office before heading to the airport. He was glad at least the chaplain visited him this morning. He missed not having a whole pack of grandkids like some of his other friends. His son died. He only had one granddaughter. That was it. And he had secretly or not-so-secretly feared that would be the end of the Wiggins bloodline.

When Emma told him she was engaged, he jumped at his opportunity when the chaplain came to visit him later that day. He mentioned to her about how excited he was that she was getting married and wished, since the doctors told him he was doing a little better, that he could just see her get married. Just like Mr. H's daughter got married in the hospital room. It was his dream. His deep desire. He longed for the opportunity to see his granddaughter, his only living flesh, move forward with her life in a holy union.

He chuckled sheepishly at his earlier gaffe.

"So, tell me more about this wedding. You must be so excited," the chaplain continued.

"Oh, well, you know, Emma has been quite hush-hush about all the details. I mean, I didn't even know she was serious about this fellow until she told me this week, after Mr. H's daughter got married." He shook his head as he picked up a child-size carton of juice from his breakfast tray.

The chaplain smiled and helped him to peel back the foil on top so he could poke the straw through. She was glad he was feeling more strong today. That he wanted to touch anything from his meal tray, unlike some of the other mornings she had visited him. She told him earlier that she noticed how much he had perked up since news of the wedding. Her smile was wide and sincere.

"But she told me he's such a nice fellow, that chap. I just hope he treats my little Emma good. The way she deserves to be treated. You know? She's a good girl, she is. She's all I've got." He leaned his head back and took a sip of the apple juice from the carton forgoing the straw. He had yanked it out earlier. For some reason, he just found it awkward to slurp through it. He was never much of a straw man he would say.

"Aw. I'm sure he will, Mr. Wiggins." The chaplain smiled wide again. Mr. Wiggins noticed how pearly white her teeth were. Sparkling. He remembered how his own teeth were when he had them. He remembered quite a lot these days.

He spent so much time on his own between Emma's visits that he had a whole lot of time to ponder stuff.

"So, she's off to New York this morning, you mentioned."

"Yes. Yes." He paused for a moment to give it thought. His eyes were suddenly downcast. "I will miss her. Not sure if she left yet or not. Hold on a minute." Mr. Wiggins reached over to the side table and picked up a piece of paper from the counter top. "She gave me her work number to call if anything came up. I think she said she and her fiancé will be leaving from there."

The chaplain adjusted herself in her seat. She noticed Mr. Wiggins had a bit of difficulty reading the numbers on the keypad to dial. His fingers were slightly shaky.

"Would you like me to help?" she offered gently, trying hard not to impose on his independence. She understood how important it was for him. She knew enough from her earlier visits and from what she read about him in his patient chart how much it meant to him and how he would get anxious if he felt anyone was trying to downplay his abilities. Dignity. That's all he wanted.

"Sure. Why not?" He hesitated first, before agreeing.

The chaplain carefully dialled the numbers based on what was scribbled down on the note. She keyed the numbers in 555-1200.

"Good morning, Fletcher Advertising," Lucinda's cheery voice came through the phone.

The chaplain introduced herself and told her that Mr. Wiggins was on the phone. She handed the phone to him and then he took over.

"Yes, good morning. Is Emma there, please?"

"Oh, I'm sorry, you've just missed them. She left already with-" Lucinda stopped herself. Though it was Emma's grandfather and she knew a little about his situation, she had to respect company privacy policy. She was about to divulge too much information for a receptionist.

Mr. Wiggins sounded disappointed then shifted his tone of voice. "Well, I'll speak to her when she gets back from New York with her fiancé then."

"Excuse me?" Lucinda sounded shocked. Puzzled. Perhaps she hadn't heard Mr. Wiggins correctly. He must learn to speak up when talking on the phone, he thought to himself.

"Her fiancé. Evan." He emphasized and enunciated with more clarity, his voice volume cranked up a notch. "She's with Evan, right?"

"Yes," Lucinda responded slowly with an air of what sounded like shock to Mr. Wiggins. He fobbed it off.

"When Emma gets back from New York with her fiancé Evan, please tell her I'll call her." He exhaled sharply.

When Mr. Wiggins hung up the phone, he shook his head, grinned at the chaplain, and tsked. "These people. Hard of hearing. Too much loud music probably."

The chaplain smiled.

When Lucinda got off the phone with Emma's grandfather, she'd thought that was the strangest call she'd ever received.

Emma?

Evan?

Fiancé?

What the hell did I miss?

Her eyes narrowed as she gaped at the vacant double door leading to reception—where Emma and Evan just walked through to head to the airport. Together. The wheels in her head spun madly.

Just what the hell is going on?

She glanced at the Rolodex on her desk and immediately started to flip through it for a phone number.

10

"So. You had breakfast?" Evan glanced at Emma as they made their way through the airport terminal. They had already checked in and were through airport security.

"Actually, I didn't have time this morning."

"Good. Let's go grab something to eat over here." He still looked appealing, Emma thought, even though he had his bag slung over his shoulder with his laptop in it. He had on his shades which made him look, oh, so hot!

They made their way over to a café near their boarding gate and sat down after Evan eyed a nice spot by the window looking into the terminal. It had a comfy booth. Private. They had at least forty minutes prior to boarding the plane. They had arrived extra early and the flight was already delayed.

"So, what are you two having today?" the cheerful young waitress asked as she approached them. It was certainly a fancier-than-most café in the airport. One glance at the menu and Emma was sure it was one of the more upscale cafés for sure. The prices were through the roof. Still, the cosy environment and dim lit lights made the atmosphere more than comfortable.

They ordered a full breakfast with two coffees, scrambled eggs, bacon, sausage, and hotcakes on the side with Canadian maple syrup. Emma thought of her mother at that instant for some reason.

Her mouth watered. Her stomach grumbled. She hoped Evan could not hear it through her belly. But with all the noise in the restaurant, the clanking of dishes in adjacent eateries, and the constant overhead paging, she'd think not.

"All set for your first big client trip?" Evan turned his attention to her. His eyes were sparkling, dark, sexy. She really needed to stop conjuring visions of him.

Naked.

In her bed.

Beside her.

No, the seductive ambiance of the café didn't help much. She had to remember to keep at the forefront of her mind, he's my boss. My boss. Nothing more. Nothing less.

"Oh, definitely. I'm really looking forward to the challenge. I think it would be fabulous to get the campaign going this month. Being spring and everything and ahead of the busy June month of weddings."

Evan nodded in agreement.

They began talking about the shoot, what to expect, the client, and their trip to New York.

Emma secretly hoped they would be able to get in a little bit of sightseeing before they departed the Big Apple. She just couldn't go all that way and not get a little tour of the landmarks, the hotspots. She hadn't been to New York since she was nine-years-old and didn't even remember what it was like. She'd visited a cousin in the early days and only had memories of their sweeping estate in Long Island.

She just had to go to Times Square. She'd noticed that the headquarters of Weddings R Us was not that far from Times Square in lower Manhattan—New York's famous island.

She was excited, giddy almost, just thinking about her business trip. Of all the places, of all the clients, she'd really lucked out by having her new client's head office in the heart of New York.

The meal had finally arrived. Talk about fast, attentive service.

After offering a quick, whispered grace, Emma dug in to her tray.

"You know, that's what I love about you." Evan sat grinning at her as she took a mouthful of scrambled eggs into her mouth. She couldn't swallow.

"Excuse me?" she responded, puzzled.

The word "love" came out of his beautiful curved lips followed by the word "you." Was she hearing things all of a sudden? Could there be a more perfect combination of words?

"I notice that you always say your grace before you eat. Even in a fast food joint. You're not afraid to show your gratitude. Remarkable. Just so you know, many people don't do that. Not these days." His voice was deep and low. Seductive. Very relaxed. She didn't think she could help herself now. She really wanted to reach over and hug and squeeze him. She noticed lovers over by the next booth and wished to goodness they were not travelling on business but as lovers going to the Big Apple for some fun. Passion.

She didn't know how to respond. She felt self-conscious more than anything. She really needed to work on accepting compliments more readily. Wait a minute, had he been watching her during their business lunches together, even when they were in a group? God, he was observant. She tried to be discreet about saying grace in public. Not that she was hiding it, of course. Just not to be so obvious about it.

"Thanks," she uttered and blushed. She really didn't know how she would finish her breakfast. She was glad he suggested having a full breakfast at the café, since most domestic flights, especially on short trips, didn't serve meals. Not even snacks these days.

Evan shovelled in a mouthful of his eggs and sausage as he listened for their boarding call. His eyes glanced around. There were others eating quickly and laughing, talking. When his eyes travelled to the far window where he could see the airplanes lined up, he was thankful the sky was clear, blue, and bright. He loved travelling when the weather was stable. Not that a little turbulence turned him off flying. He merely hated long delays, landing in strange cities until the weather or storm cleared up in the destination where he would be close to landing.

He had travelled to enough cities as part of his job to know. He'd been there, done that.

The aroma of bacon and eggs in the café dominated the environment. The taste of sausage in his mouth was juicy. He felt the coolness of the café, oddly the air conditioner was probably on.

He saw out the window to the terminal gates passengers wheeling their hand luggage behind them, some carrying children. Travellers dressed in casual wear lugging bags and cameras and their boarding passes, hurrying to meet their flights. He loved the whole travelling gig. It made him feel like he was going places.

He remembered when he was young, his family didn't have much money to travel. He used to look up at the sky at night and see what he first thought was a travelling star but as he closely observed the strobe-light flashes, he realised it was an aircraft going to where—he didn't know. He wished he could travel often.

Something about being up in the air.

Travelling. Going far. Going places. New. Exciting. Different.

Then his eyes peeled back on the vision of loveliness before him. Sweet Emma Wiggins. She was something, wasn't she?

Talk about travelling to new, exciting places. He really wanted to explore this beautiful territory called Emma. What was she really about? Up until now, he really hadn't given it much thought. But there was just something so striking about her. Her charm, charisma, wit, delicate manners, inner-strength. He loved it all.

Especially the way she cared.

About her work.

About people.

About doing the right thing.

And about him.

She really went the extra mile and he appreciated it. He also was taken aback but at the same time, impressed by her willingness to make the last days her grandfather had on this Earth as memorable as possible by granting his last wish—however strange that may be. Of course, it was a complicated wish, since it involved someone else. He cringed at the whole marriage bit though. He knew it still wasn't for him, but he was willing to fake it to make her grandfather happy—heck, who was he kidding? He was doing it for her. Plain and simple.

"So, you have everything in place for our pending nuptials?" He grinned in her direction.

He watched as she spooned another bite of breakfast between her lips. With an edge of embarrassment, again his private domain jumped. What was it with her? Those lips. So full. So defined. He couldn't get those out of his mind.

He wondered what it would be like to get close to those soft lips of hers.

Why haven't I made a move on her before?

Oh, yeah, right! I'm her boss.

There were policies against stuff like that. Besides, she was clearly professional and he had to respect that. Not like she was the flirting type. Not like some of the other secretaries or previous receptionists who would throw themselves at his feet, dress inappropriately for the office, and flirt openly with him and such.

No, Emma was very sweet, kind, professional. He respected her efficiency and her high level of professionalism. Besides, he knew of an acquaintance who made out with an employee, and when that went sour as sometimes these things do, boy, did it bite him in the butt. He got slapped with a heavy sexual harassment suit. That really did in his career. Not to mention his reputation. Something Evan cared a lot about. He dated a lot of women, but few of them he worked with. He really didn't want to travel down that path.

He noticed Emma hesitate at first. "The arrangements are in place. Gramps, I mean, my grandfather had spoken to the chaplain at the hospital and she said she'd be more than happy to perform the ceremony. She's fully licensed." Emma sighed and paused.

"Everything okay?" Evan dropped his fork on his plate and leaned closer to Emma.

Emma exhaled sharply. She counted to three, dropped her fork on her plate then spoke. "Evan, there's been something I've been meaning to tell you."

His sexy dark, cinnamon-colored eyes gazed directly into her eyes, waiting. This didn't help with her nerves, of course. She felt her belly flutter inside. Heat rose high in her chest to her throat. She felt her throat would soon constrict under the pressure. But she sucked in another deep breath.

"It's regarding my grandfather. You know, he really wanted to see me walk down the aisle. It meant the world to him, so—"

"Can I have your attention, please?" The overhead pager came on loud, both instinctively froze and narrowed their eyes to listen for their gate number.

"Flight 98 is ready to board at gate six. Will passengers please report to gate six?"

They both finished their meals and grabbed their bags to head over to the gate. Luckily, the café was a few steps from the boarding gate.

Emma's heart thumped. Maybe it was for a good reason she was interrupted from telling Evan he was about to be a real groom next week, not a fake.

Maybe she should just wait until they've met with the client and sorted out the ad shoot, and maybe catch a bit of the New York scene before heading back to Texas. Everything happened for a reason. She remembered her grandmother telling her when she was little.

In fact, Grandma would always drum that and Ecclesiastics "to everything there is a season" in her head while growing up so that she wouldn't feel too depressed or be too hard on herself with all the disappointments and heartbreaks she'd endured when she was younger. Stuff like her parents' divorce, changing schools as often as she changed her mood, her father's death...and now...?

Evan didn't seem too bothered with what she was about to say. Maybe he thought she was just tossing in a little small talk after answering his question to eat up a chunk of time before they boarded so their meal conversation wouldn't be too quiet between them. Evan pulled out his wallet to pay the bill that the waitress had left on the table. He left the amount of their breakfasts including a generous tip, Emma noticed. She also noted that he didn't take a copy of the receipt to expense it for their business trip. After all, they would bill the client since it was her idea to get the ad agency out to New York to supervise the first major ad shoot.

"Oh, you left the receipt." Emma scurried back over to the table but her hand was stopped from reaching for the piece of paper on the table by Evan's. He touched her hand so gently, butterflies definitely let loose in her belly just then. His skin was smooth, delicate, soft, yet well toned. She felt moisture on her own hand. Why did he have that kind of effect on her?

"It's okay. I've got it." His silky voice was deep, sexy. His smile was dimpled and seductive as he peered deeply into her eyes. He sure was making a lot of serious eye-contact with her lately, she noticed. But she didn't feel uncomfortable.

Not at all. Just nervous. Good nervous.

Was he flirting with her? Maybe that was her imagination, too! She smiled back and said, "Thanks for a yummy breakfast." It certainly was ultra delicious and by far the most expensive breakfast she'd had in her life to that point.

They hurried over to the passenger boarding lounge, and since they were travelling first class, they had the luxury of boarding first.

"I'm surprised you booked us on business class," she commented, smiling sheepishly when they arrived at their seats Aisle 3, Seats A and B. She'd never travelled first class, executive class, or business class before. The plush blue seats were cushioned amply. They appeared more like oversized recliner chairs that you see in infomercials. And the leg space. God, there was a whole lot of leg room. Looked more like a living area lounge than a seating area on an aircraft, especially a domestic flight. She noticed the power ports located between the large space between the passenger seats (or sofas, she mused to herself). She loved the newness of the cabin design. She assessed there was plenty of room for working. Lights were mounted on the seat backs to illuminate the work table in addition to the overhead light. She noticed the ten inch touch-screen tilting monitors. Each passenger had his own. When she got situated, she looked at the interlocking tray tables. She was impressed with the innovative design. She had two tables. One that dropped down from the seat back of the passenger in front of her and the other lifted from the center console.

Unbelievable.

She was used to being crammed into coach class where you barely had room to breathe much less move your feet. The passenger seat in front seemed to be so in-your-face compared to this. And when the passenger in front, God forbid, leaned back, well, there goes your personal space. You just had no choice but to lean back too. But this? This was nice. She loved the privacy and comfort of the upper class cabin on the plane.

So this is what if feels like to be well off.

Only the super rich, affluent, or successful business people could afford to travel like this *all* the time.

"It's your first client trip. Wanted it to be special for you. Enjoy it while you can." He smiled and cocked his eyebrow to her.

"Aw. Thanks, Evan. That's so…sweet of you." She could not believe he took great thought into the fact that this would be her first client trip, heck, her first official company expensed business trip. She was really soaring in life—she smiled at the pun.

He lugged her hand luggage to the overhead compartment before stowing his own. He ensured the bags were tucked in properly before slamming the compartment door shut above her head. His biceps flexed well, Emma noted, when he lifted the bags.

God, she loved his physique. She also noticed when he had lifted up his arms to place the bags above her that he had rock hard abs through his t-shirt.

She felt herself get hot again. She loosened her cardigan. She had to stop admiring the man, or she wasn't going to be able to think straight or do anything right. Just to think, they'd be taking vows next week—though he didn't believe it would be for real. Okay, she had to really get back to reality.

She stared out the window and saw other Boeings docked at their gate bay. All domestic flights. Then she looked around the nice cabin area again. The flight attendants seemed extra courteous, treating her more like a celeb than a common passenger. They called her Ms. Wiggins. She guessed they knew everybody by name in first class or business class. These seats certainly come with something. They didn't come cheap at all. She'd probably have to put away a month's salary to cover the cost of a one-way business class or first class ticket.

"The seats are ergonomically advanced, by the way," Evan commented, noticing her gaze in awe.

"Nice." She nodded, a tinge of embarrassment evident on her face. She really didn't want him to think that she'd totally never clued into this type of stuff before. She had a decent upbringing. Maybe not exposed to the lifestyle of the rich and famous, but she was not doing too bad. You would think she wasn't raised with indoor plumbing or electricity the way he acted. Not that it would be a disgrace. Her grandparents were so poor they hadn't seen that type of life before they immigrated as children to America with their parents.

"The seats can also recline completely flat," he continued.

Okay, now I'm really impressed.

She nodded thoughtfully, as if what he was saying was nice, but not *that* impressive.

"There's also, I believe, a choice of thirty-five feature movies and up to eighteen hours of pre-loaded television shows, fifty music CDs, fifteen games and fourteen audio channels. You can pretty much view what ever you like." He demonstrated to her as he showed her the equipment.

"That's…wow! Awesome." She smiled as she fidgeted with her new gadget.

She was oblivious to the sound of chatter and murmurs from the other passengers boarding the plane and making their ways to their own seats. Her eyes drank in the view of the beautiful landscape of the runway in the distance. Her ears took in the sound of the airplane engine. That piercing, airy sound.

Endless personalised entertainment? Cosy space? Now this was a good way to travel.

After take-off, Emma got comfy into her recliner. She really wanted to snuggle into something—or with someone else. And he was sitting right beside her. Good thing God designed mortals so their thoughts would be private. Inside their own heads.

Evan flipped open his laptop and powered it on when it was safe to do so, right after the captain of the plane announced passengers may proceed with their equipment.

He opened up the Weddings R Us folder in his client folder and proceeded with one of the client files.

"What's that?" Emma turned to him after pulling down the shade of her oval window to block out the bright sun. They were already at the altitude above the clouds. She could almost feel the warmth of the sun beaming through the window, if that were at all possible.

"Just working on some last minute details." He seemed focused on the file he opened. His eyebrows furrowed. He placed his hand on his chin in thought.

"Something wrong?" Emma leaned over to see his screen. Guess there were advantages and disadvantages to being in business class. She had to lean over very far to get a glimpse of his computer screen since the seats were spaced out farther than in coach class.

"Just- Not sure if I wanna go along with this image." His attention was still transfixed on the laptop screen.

She took a good look. "You know, we could always change it up a little." She noticed the woman in the mock ad. "We could use a variety of nationalities, cultures. Give it a universal appeal."

He nodded. "True." They knew they had to work along with the client and give her what she wanted, but it was also their own judgment call to present enticing suggestions.

"I thought we could even go along a few backdrops. In fact..." Emma's voice octave increased. He could tell she was getting excited. "We could include an image of a Greek wedding, African wedding, American wedding..."

"I see your point." He gestured and flipped over to another screen and typed something.

"We could get different models from different backgrounds. Weddings R Us is about universality. The U can be emphasized like that." He could tell Emma's excitement grew. "We could merge the U in the ad into Universality and have the cultures merge into one."

"Sort of like that Michael Jackson video, Black or White."

He smiled. "Yep. Sort of like that. Within a more reasonable budget, of course."

He loved the way they bounced ideas off each other. It was as if she could read his mind and turn up on the same page as his direction of thought. He loved her for it. Heck, he was loving more things about her every day.

But he wasn't going to go there. He didn't want to confuse professionalism and commendable work ethics with anything more.

He couldn't wait to land in New York and get this show off the ground.

The flight was surprisingly smooth and flew by, so to speak. Emma peeked out of her window to see the beautiful city of dreams.

New York!

The city that hardly ever slept. Ever. The pilot had welcomed them to New York and announced the weather was partly cloudy, high of 74 degrees Fahrenheit with a slight chance of rain. Wind speed of three miles per hour.

LaGuardia airport was close to Manhattan central which made it one of the more popular airports. The airport was located on the beautiful waterfront of Flushing Bay and Bowery Bay.

The view of the waters was calming. There was something about being near a body of water that soothed her. Though it was an overcast, she saw some sun peek through the clouds to illuminate the beauty of the still water below as they prepared for landing.

Emma was just a child when she first visited. She didn't remember any of it from then. Now she recalled it was named after a very popular, former mayor of New York.

In fact, the ninety-ninth New York City mayor. An Italian by the name of Fiorello Henry La Guardia. Emma remembered reading somewhere that La Guardia Airport was actually voted the "greatest airport in the world" by the worldwide aviation community in the early 1960s.

They sped through baggage claims with no trouble and headed out to one of New York's famous yellow taxi stands. Their intended destination was recorded by the cheery dispatcher on site and they headed to the hotel drinking in a good view of the Big Apple on their way to lower Manhattan.

A far cry from the plains of small town Mercy Springs, Texas. She was definitely in urban surroundings. There were so much distinction with the older, characteristic buildings in New York. Emma noticed a lot of construction sites over buildings as they drove through to the hotel. A lot of architectural facelifts were underway.

She loved the mixture of new designs to the buildings erected in the last century, the early 1930s and so on. It was an awesome blend to see the different grey, brown-coloured fixtures. She really couldn't wait to soak in some of the tourist attractions once they had some free time. Presuming they had any!

When they arrived on 45th Street to reach their hotel, near Broadway and 45th Street, she was in awe of being near the famous Broadway.

Just outside the hotel, Emma soaked in the midtown Manhattan view. Buildings were dressed with all these elaborate digital or poster advertisements. This city was certainly an advertiser's dream.

As Evan spoke with the porters and arranged for their luggage, she took in the enormously tall billboard ads on the buildings and theatres nearby. The Phantom of the Opera, Lion King, South Pacific, the Sound of Music, Shrek. Every show she could imagine was playing somewhere nearby. She almost wanted to regress into a little school girl again. "Oh, please! Please, take me to the show," she pretty much wanted to beg.

There were crowds of colorful people everywhere. Business executives, show people, tourists, you name it. She was close to Times Square Studios, home of Good Morning, America, MTV's New York studios, The Hard Rock Café, Planet Hollywood, and Rockefeller Center to name a few. And she just had to visit Madame Tussauds Wax Museum.

And of course, she caught a glimpse of the famous tower at number One Times Square where over a million people gathered every year at New Year's Eve to watch the ball drop. Many bright ads including the bigger-than-life Coca-Cola digital ad glowed from the tower.

Amazing!

To see it up close in person was a whole new ballgame. Emma thought the people of New York were so lucky to have so many beautiful landmarks and world-famous attractions.

She could see now why they called it the city that never sleeps. She couldn't imagine having the time to snooze with so much going on. She once read that you could spend a lifetime in New York and not see everything, even if you stayed awake twenty-four hours in the day.

You just could not be in one of the most elaborate entertainment districts of the world and not be overtaken by its fascinating features. She didn't mind the sound of the honking traffic, the laughter, the noise of busy travellers, or people on their way to work.

It must be a dream to work around here, she mused.

She could not believe her luck, as she was in one of the most glamorous theatre districts in the world and right beside the famous Times Square. Times Square was *the* major intersection in Manhattan to be. A commercial district right there at the junction between Broadway and Seventh Avenue.

"Geez, no wonder they call it the 'crossroads of the world,'" she commented as she soaked in the spectaculars. There were so many large animated digital advertisements outside.

The marble floor of the hotel's entrance glimmered with the glow of the lights above. It looked as if you could see your reflection in it. She loved the beautiful, elaborate floral arrangements on the table in the lobby. For some reason, wedding bells went off in her mind.

She noticed farther down by the check-in counter a nice plush, red carpet where many people stood around, some sitting on the comfortable lounge chairs waiting for their loved one or for service with their luggage by their side. Some on their cell phones making calls. Others paced with their hands in their pockets. Waiting. Some were flipping through brochures of shows in town—probably on Broadway.

She noticed other travellers with their bags either checking in or out. But she was checking out the plush furniture, the cosy feel with the dim lights and the tall ceiling with the enormous chandelier above.

While the pleasant clerk checked them in, Evan turned to Emma and told her there was a message from Lucinda at FAC. Puzzled, Emma took the note. Scrawled on it was a message.

"Not to worry. Your grandfather called the office today."

She swallowed hard. Why would he call? She was going to call the palliative care unit once she got into her suite and powered on her cell phone.

They got checked in and Evan picked up their electronic key cards and headed up the elevator to the twentieth floor.

Their rooms were situated side by side. They knew they didn't have time to waste. The client meeting would be in a hour, which didn't give them much time. Luckily, lunch would be served at the Weddings R Us office.

When Emma opened up her hotel suite, she paused in awe at the window where the drapes were drawn back to expose the outside world.

The view was breathtaking. Both she and Evan got a good view of the heavily populated, dazzling entertainment district of Times Square and the large poster ads of various theatre shows. The flashing digital ad lights were intriguing. She thought it would be sparkling at night time to catch the view. When she moved closer to the window, she could see herds of yellow taxi cabs below making their way through traffic.

Was it always this busy in New York? At any given time of the week?

She dialled her grandfather's hospital room extension. "Gramps?" She thought the phone had been answered. But she was wrong.

Evan came to her door and asked if everything was okay with her grandfather. "No news yet. Didn't get an answer. I'll call Lucinda to see if there's more to the message."

Evan's cell phone buzzed. He excused himself to answer it. Emma told him it was okay to go back to his suite. She would catch up with him soon once she unpacked.

"Good afternoon, Fletcher Advertising," Lucinda answered the phone.

"Hey, Lucinda. It's Emma, you left a message."

"Oh, right." For some strange reason, Lucinda seemed different. As if she knew something. As if she knew a secret.

Emma could tell by her tone of voice. Now she wondered in a panic, what exactly did Gramps say to Lucinda? Did he mention the wedding next week?

Oh, God, Emma hoped not. Feared not. Her grandfather had been gleefully telling every single person

SHADONNA RICHARDS

he met and spoke to that his granddaughter was getting
married next week to the president of an ad agency.

She clasped her head to her forehead. She just
couldn't warn him beforehand not to breathe a word to a
single living soul. Then again, she wished maybe she
should have. She thought it would seem strange. Odd.
Bizarre. Almost as bizarre as her plan to get married next
week to a gamophobic.

There was an uncomfortable silence on the phone.
What was she playing at? Emma wondered as she crossed
one arm around her chest and narrowed her eyes looking
out the hotel window at the Coca-Cola digital ad on the
Times Square tower.

"He's fine. He just wanted to see if he could tell
you two to have a nice trip," Lucinda said, snapping her
lips chewing gum.

Ooh, Emma really disliked that. First of all, she
ought to tell Lucinda, it was very rude for a receptionist to
be chewing gum but she should already know that by now.
Secondly, she wanted to ask just what the hell she was
playing at.

She sensed a very cocky tone of voice when
Lucinda knew it was Emma calling. Or was she just
suffering the effects of some serious jetlag followed by
non-sleep from last night? She thanked Lucinda politely
and hung up the phone.

No way was she going to give her any kind of
satisfaction by revealing any details. She didn't care at that
point what Lucinda thought. Though she could hear
Lucinda striking some sort of rumour about she and Evan
and her recent promotion.

Evan's knock on her door jolted her back to
reality. She had other hurdles to heave over right now,
thank you very much. One of them, at the moment, was to
make her new client…very happy.

11

The taxi cab drove them to Greenwich Village not too far from the hotel where Emma spotted a row of brownstone buildings. As they pulled up to the curb and got out, Evan paid and tipped the cab driver handsomely.

"You ready?" He looked at her with an air of concern. He noticed she kept raking her fingers through her hair. She only did this when she was nervous about something. Very nervous.

"Ready as can be." Her feigned chuckle was fraught with tension.

Evan thought she had a lot on her mind, probably something to do with her grandfather. He began to wonder if it was a good idea making her come to New York, knowing that her grandfather's condition could change in a heartbeat. So to speak. Too late for that now.

They ended up at a nice corner unit. A 10,000 square foot, four-story brownstone office building probably built in the late 1800s by the look of the design.

Emma noticed the first floor was beautifully renovated with plush facilities. A restaurant was located on the main floor.

When she saw the brownstones on the street, memories flooded her mind, even though she'd never lived in one. She thought of the popular television shows The Cosby Show and Sesame Street and even one of the characters from Sex and the City who lived in one. She even recalled that Breakfast at Tiffany's, starring Audrey Hepburn, most of the film took place in the brownstone apartment building.

Of course, many of these brownstones were converted into offices and eateries. In the buildings themselves no doubt unique characters lived and had stories of their own. She would love to do more research on that.

They made their way up through the lavish reception to the second floor. Again, beautiful, high-tech renovation surrounded them. There, on the door the sign read:

WEDDINGS R US.

Founded by Herbert and Kelsia Endo

She wanted to offer at a later date to redesign their logo, if they were receptive to it. It seemed oddly basic and formal for what image they wanted to portray.

They had lunch with the client at a gorgeously designed Chinese gourmet restaurant. The aroma of baked entrees tantalised Emma's taste buds. Her mouth watered. She hadn't eaten since their elaborate breakfast at the gourmet airport café in Texas before they departed.

She ordered the orange chicken, a crispy chicken battered, stir fried and flavoured with orange peel sauce with a side order of assorted vegetable steamed and served in sauce and a cup of boiled rice on the side. Evan ordered an exotic dish of beef with black bean sauce and broccoli sliced tender and mixed in a tasty sauce. The clients ordered similar dishes.

The business late luncheon went better than expected. The client was impressed with Evan and Emma's new concept for the direction of the ad campaign. As a matter-of-fact, they loved the idea. Especially the usually stoic, hard-to-please Ms. Endo.

Later, they headed down to the studio off 46th Street to supervise the shoot they had already discussed. It was for a wedding scene with a bride and groom and a few family members in the background to give it that whole traditional appeal.

The studio was dark inside except for the bright overhead illumination that shined above. The lights were directed on to a screen where the models would be posing for the initial shoot.

A woman with purple hair gelled into a Mohawk, thick black eye-liner, pierced nose, and black skin-tight outfit rushed out from the back as she shook her hands up in the air. By the looks of her, she would be a hair or makeup artist.

"This is unbelievable. I can't believe this."

"What is it?" Ms. Endo looked appalled.

"Our bride model. She's sick. Throwing up. She can't do the shoot. I think she pregnant or something."

Ms. Endo rolled her eyes. "This is unacceptable. The art team is here all the way from Texas. They're only in town for a couple of days. We need to get this thing moving right away. Find a replacement!" She rolled the words off her tongue with such a shrilling sound, Emma thought her ear drums would pierce.

Just then, the presumed-to-be makeup artist eyed Emma from head to toe and took great care in tracing her silhouette. Emma shifted uncomfortably on the spot.

"Why not her?" The cosmetologist turned her eyes back to Ms. Endo.

"But she's from the ad agency."

"And…she seems to have the right measurements." She smiled. "I've been doing makeup, costume, and hair for years to know a replacement when I see one."

Evan stepped forward and leaned towards Emma with a grin. "How do you feel about that? Why not?" he whispered in her ear. Emma thought she would melt. Why not? Maybe she should have a go at it.

Evan spent the next twenty minutes talking with the client while Emma was backstage getting made up for the bridal shoot. His hands behind his back, head tilted, Ms. Endo seemed to be enjoying his attention as well as the conversation.

He was not prepared for what happened next.

A vision of beauty.

Emma, dressed up in a bridal dress. He felt his manhood rise. He stopped breathing.

She was, in a word, breathtaking.

Literally.

He couldn't speak. For the first time in his life, he was dumbfounded. He must have stopped mid-sentence when speaking to Ms. Endo. But he was oblivious to that fact now.

They say that a dress can make a woman, but he believed Emma gave life to her ensemble. She shined in it.

She wore a gorgeous satin royal bridal gown with an elaborate plunging neckline that accentuated her full breasts. The dress had an embroidered and beaded bodice with a slight drop princess line waist that once again showed off her finest assets, in Evan's opinion. Her gorgeous mane of beautiful, ebony curls were swept up into a French ponytail accentuating her high cheekbones and defining lips and eyes.

She was stunning.

It's amazing what they did with her makeup to highlight her already natural attractiveness.

Evan was sure he salivated while eyeing her. But he couldn't help himself. What man could? He couldn't peel his eyes off her. He didn't want to. He was mesmerised. Intrigued. Hypnotised by her beauty. Not just her exterior—she glowed from within. Her grace. Her humility. Her demeanor. It was everything. *She* was everything.

Was this what if felt like to fall in love?

He needed emotional CPR. His heart just stopped. He didn't know if he could go on without telling her how he really felt. But there was an anchor above his head, and he didn't want it to fall and destroy everything that could be. Never mind the fact that she was his employee and they were there strictly on business. But that Fletcher curse was real and true, even if it sounded strange or bizarre to mention it. He had to stop himself from falling in love with her. That may be a feat impossible to master.

Emma noticed Evan didn't speak. Did she look *that*…awkward? She sure felt awkward. Her heart beat fast and hard. The photographer, lights, studio team, and Evan made her feel self-conscious.

Say something, silly!

"You look beautiful." Evan's silky voice was deep and seductive. Oh, God, did he just read her mind? Was it that obvious? Ms. Endo looked at Evan then at Emma and back again. Oh, no. Was it that blatantly obvious? Emma hoped Ms. Endo didn't clue into the sexual tension in the room between she and Evan. She hoped not. Horror struck her at the thought. She straightened her expression and perched a humble smile back onto her face to prep for the shoot. She felt moist in different areas of her body all of a sudden. The last thing she wanted to do was ruin her newly done up makeup. She had to hand it to Lilly, the makeup artist, she really knew her stuff.

Immediately, Ms. Endo started fussing over Emma and even went as far as to place her hands on Emma's breasts to readjust them in her dress. Ever conscious of Evan watching, Emma flushed. Heat rushed inside her.

After the wildly successful photo shoot in the studio, the group moved to Times Square to take a few dazzling, live snapshots with an entertaining background. A bride in the middle of one of the world's busiest entertainment districts.

The artistic contrast would make quite a statement. Basically, it didn't matter whether you were in the country, down South, upstate, or on a ranch. Weddings R Us catered to all brides, in all situations, from all localities.

Evan was famished and wanted to take Emma to dinner once they got back to the hotel. It was early in the evening, and they dined on the patio overlooking Manhattan. The night lights glowed. They enjoyed each other's company and talked about the shoot, the ad campaign, and weddings.

"You really looked…look amazing." He gazed into her eyes and could tell she was nervous. They sat on the rooftop, the breeze gently rustling Emma's long, silky head of curls.

She held her gaze on her plate, chewing carefully now, he noticed. "Thanks. So do you."

Emma took in another bite of her gourmet dinner while she sat at a candlelit table opposite her sexy boss.

She looked out at the beautiful sunset sky that was turning a remarkable shade of red and purple.

The glittering lights of the Big Apple dazzled her as she overlooked the busy district below. She wondered if now would be the best time to tell Evan about their not-so-fake wedding nuptials next week. But she hesitated as she was aware of his eyes on her. She really didn't want to ruin a good mood—just in case.

Not now.

After dinner, Evan suggested they take in the sights of the Big Apple. "There's a tour bus leaving soon." He glanced at his watch as they walked out of the lobby of the main floor of the multi-level gourmet restaurant. They walked out onto the cool, New York street.

"At this time? I thought the tour buses only ran in the daytime." She looked so cute with her puzzled, innocent expression.

"Are you kidding me? New York is the city that never sleeps—remember?" He grinned as he reached over and squeezed her shoulder. "Besides, the best time to see New York is at night. With all the lights and everything. I think the tour ends at eight, anyway."

They walked on as a couple. Evan felt good that she didn't mind holding his arm as they strolled on 45th Street back to the hotel. She was beginning to feel more relaxed with him. At times, he wished they were a couple, but then he dismissed the idea. It was probably for the best that they weren't for professional as well as personal reasons. Not far from the entrance of the hotel, they saw the green double decker, open rooftop bus at the port. A uniformed man was outside talking to tourists. He had a ticket machine and started to wheel the device as one of the tourists handed him some money.

"We're just in time," Evan said as they approached. "How much?" he posed to the gentleman.

"It's $40 for a full tour of lower Manhattan and going to the Statue of Liberty."

"Good. Two tickets, please."

After Evan paid, he walked behind Emma as she made her way up the winding steps to the top level of the bus.

Bad idea. Very bad idea!

Evan could feel his groin area twitch as she wiggled her derriere up the steps. Emma had a perfectly round, full behind, he noticed. And that tiny waist. He needed to divert his attention quickly, before he made a fool of himself.

When they arrived on the second level of the bus, Emma pulled Evan towards the front.

"We've got the best seats in the house." She smiled.

He took in a whiff of her sweet scented perfume as the breeze blew gently. It drove him crazy. He could still see the beauty in her face. She still had the subtle makeup from the shoot earlier in the day that really accentuated her best features. Which was everything on her perfectly laid out skin. She looked glowing even as the day slowly morphed into the night.

As they drove off, the tour guide, a friendly, cheerful, humorous, older African American gentleman, welcomed everyone on the bus and announced the trip of their life. He told them his name was Chet and went on to explain the stops ahead then proceeded onward to see them firsthand. Emma snuggled into Evan's arms as they drove down 45th Avenue towards their destination. That move caught him by surprise. Was she starting to cling to him? Maybe it was the whole atmosphere of the day, the mood of the hour, and being in New York.

"You know, I was just thinking of that song," she declared.

"What song?"

"Oh, nothing."

"No, tell me." He grinned wider as the wind blew his hair at the speed of the bus.

He could see her face flush with embarrassment. It looked as if she spoke something she didn't mean to.

"Well, it's just, you know, this old song. I think it's called Arthur's Theme. When you get caught between the moon and New York City…"

"The best that you can do is…fall in love?" He grinned.

"You're something else, you know. Are you saying you're falling in love?" He grinned.

"With the city. With the city."

She pouted, embarrassment could just knock her over, he thought as he grinned to himself. God, she looked so cute with that sexy little pout of hers, accentuating her full, defined, raspberry colored lips.

Well, at least he remembered the tune, his grandmother used to play it all the time, some 80s song.

He looked up and could see the dark blue sky with the broad streak of redness of the sunset and the half moon above glowing above the skyscrapers. This moment was almost perfect.

He inched in closer to Emma. He wondered if this were a bad idea. He really didn't want to lead her on. Evan had to remind himself this was a business trip and this was a professional experience.

He looked around. The tour bus was pretty full considering it was well into the evening. He'd guessed right that the night bus tours were just as popular as the daytime ones.. It was too damn romantic coming here and doing this. What on earth was he thinking?

Chet announced on his handheld microphone that they'd arrived at Greenwich Village and proceeded to tell the passengers about the colorful history of the place. Next up was Times Square where they learned fascinating facts. They enjoyed seeing the lights of the buildings, especially the world famous Empire State Building, which was at one point in history, the tallest building in the world.

They drove past the Flatiron Building, Union Square, Soho, Chinatown, Little Italy, Lower East Side, and East Village, and Rockefeller Center on the downtown loop. They also went on the uptown loop where they passed the American Museum of Natural History and the Cathedral of St. John, the Divine, the world famous Apollo Theater, and Fifth Avenue. They scurried past Rockefeller Center and the Manhattan Bridge.

Unfortunately, the night bus tour didn't include a stop off option and Emma wished that she could also catch a day tour one day so that she could actually get to go to the places. She even wanted to pay tribute and lay flowers nearby the World Trade Center site.

Chet gave a warm smile and commented, "Looking at you two, I'd be willing to bet you're on your honeymoon. Am I right?"

Evan blushed. He chuckled nervously. How was he to answer without the risk of sounding dejected?

"We're not married," he finally said.

"What's stopping you?" Chet chuckled. "I think you two would make a fine couple."

Okay, now that was really awkward.

12

Emma wanted to interject and explain that they were getting married next week. But how could she? It was not supposed to be for real and this was not the place to announce that. Besides, you never know who else could be on the bus listening.

They both subconsciously pulled away from their comfortable body lock realising Chet had every reason to assume they were a couple. Heck, they were behaving like one.

Later, at the hotel as they walked into the lobby, they noticed people coming out of a ballroom. Loud music and laughter seemed to ricochet from the room.

"You tired?" Evan turned to Emma as they strolled on the marble floor leading to the elevator.

"Not really. D'you wanna have a look?" She gestured to the party room.

"Sure, why not?" He shrugged.

Once they had a peek at the festivities, they couldn't resist. They both enjoyed an evening of dance and entertainment at the themed night club. A live band played. Well, more like rocked the house! It was spectacular. Emma had hoped to take in a Broadway play but soon realised why New York was dubbed the city that doesn't sleep.

How could anyone get any sleep if they wanted to have fun and try everything? There was just so much to do and not enough time in the day. But heck, she was in New York and she was going to make the best of her time.

When was the last time she indulged in some rest and relaxation?

Back home in Texas, she had enough on her emotional platter.

Work.

Work.

And more work.

Taking care of her dear, sweet, ailing grandfather had really taken a toll on her and did a number on her social life or what was left of what she had. This was her time.

Guilt-free down time.

She really needed to unwind more than she realised. This was the first time in a long while she'd had fun. Real, laugh-out-loud, belly-tickly, carefree fun.

And this time, she was not ashamed or apologetic to say it felt good.

Later that evening, after they wined and dined at the dance in the ballroom, Evan and Emma walked across the hotel lobby on the plush Persian-replica rug towards the center glass elevators.

There were scores of people hanging around, laughing, talking, and mingling with each other. A scattering of some tourists with cameras took pictures before heading over to the taxi stand.

One man, who looked middle-aged, had on bright makeup and was dressed like Shirley Temple with a curly, blond wig, full red lips, and a balloon held high. The sight was something to see. His friend was also dressed up. They looked ever so cute. They resembled theatre performers. Perhaps they were just finishing up some comedy sketch. But then again, wouldn't they have been out of makeup and costume? Perhaps they had come from some themed dress-up party. It was much too early for Halloween. Still it was quite a spectacle to see.

Only in New York. Emma smiled to herself as she walked closely with Evan. The elevator doors slid open and they walked in.

"Had fun?"

"Of course, did you?" Emma held up her head to Evan, she felt somewhat mellow. Intoxicated from all the excitement of the day and the evening together.

"Course." He grinned. "You look like you could do with some sleep right about now."

"Oh, I've got all night." Emma yawned. She caught a side glimpse of Evan shaking his head and grinning.

Ding.

When they arrived to their floor, he walked her over to her door.

Evan wanted to simply kiss her on the forehead to wish her good night. But he dismissed that notion.

Too personal.

Instead, he reached over and took her hand and planted a small kiss.

"Oh." She looked surprised. Okay, probably a bad idea. He'd never touched her with a kiss before. Her caramel toned skin was smooth, silky, and soft. She oozed sensuality. She was delicate. Strong. Beautiful in every sense of the word.

"Sorry. I just…" He hesitated. He shook his head. "I don't know what got into me. I wanted to thank you for a job well done and for…" *Gracing my presence with your beautiful company this evening.* He flushed. Damn, this was not good. He was usually a man in control.

Of his emotions.
Of his feelings.
Of any situation.

Just then, she reached over and grabbed his neck gently and pulled it towards her.

She planted a warm, silky kiss on his lips.

Bad idea.

He was certainly more aroused now. It was as if there was some kind of energetic force between the two. Spiritual magnets zapping their bodies, their souls together. He just couldn't resist.

He inched closer to her. He was hard and stiff as a branch now.

She managed to open the door behind her with her electronic card key and they made their way into her suite, lips still embraced into a gracious lock as they devoured each other.

The scent of her perfume got him more excited within. He ran his fingers through her beautiful, soft, shiny curls. They felt softer than they looked. The aroma of her shampoo, so clean, vibrant, fresh.

Her lips tasted of strawberry.

They coordinated their way over to the four-poster queen sized bed in the hotel room. The drapes were already drawn. But even if the curtains were wide open, he didn't know if they'd get a chance to close them for the privacy they needed. But he didn't care.

No doubt about it, he craved her.

Desired her.

Lusted for her.

He wanted to caress her in all the places he could.

Stop.

No.

He just couldn't do it, he scolded himself. This was wrong. She was still his employee. This would all come back to bite him in the butt. Just like it did with his acquaintance.

And the curse. He'd be damned to get too involved with Emma. He was falling in love with her. And that was just a dangerous game he didn't want to play. He remembered the last time he fell in love. The curse almost took him. His ex, Gisella Trumen, smashed his heart and his dreams into a million tiny pieces while he was going to college. He almost gave up everything and nearly didn't finish his education because of the emotional mess that relationship left him in. He had yet to recover all the broken pieces of his dream. He found it hard to trust again. To give his whole heart to anyone ever again. It was just an unlucky path he did not want to tread again, at least any time soon. In his book, it was better off for some men to remain single.

Hard as it was, heart still pounding fierce in his chest, heat fully exploded in every area of his muscular body, he pulled himself off from her. He could feel the heavy pulsation in his groin area.

Damn, she looked so beautiful. He really should see a therapist. The cosmic connection between them was out of this world. What was he thinking? How much longer could he…should he keep this up?

Emma lay on the bed, dazed, puzzled.

"What?" Her chest heaved. She was breathless. "Why did you stop?"

"I need to go and take a cold shower." He did not look at her. Her eyes narrowed. Her entire body was still throbbing. Her mind was still in a fog. She'd just made out, somewhat slightly, with her boss.

But now?

He was tossing her aside? No way.

"Fine." She got up from the bed, adjusted her bra and blouse and stood up with her back turned to him. She pulled open the drapes slightly to catch a glimpse of the New York City lights.

Tears misted her eyes.

She felt him inch behind her. He wrapped his arms, gently around her waist from behind and kissed her on the top of her head. His cologne scent tantalised her nostrils. He smelled delicious.

Why was he doing this? What's wrong with him? What's wrong with her?

"I'm sorry. I didn't mean to…" His voice was too deep, throaty, and sexy that moment. She was beginning to tingle again in between her thighs. His skin felt warm and satiny. His minty breath, warm on her neck as he leaned down towards her.

"I just couldn't help myself," he continued. "You mean a lot to me. I just don't want this to get out of hand."

"What's to get out of hand?" she said as she turned around to him.

"My feelings for you. You have no idea what you do to me, do you?"

Evan could not believe what he just did. Did he just hint to his employee that he was falling in love with her?

Rule number one from the Fletcher Curse: Never admit that you are falling head over boots in love with a woman. Never let her know how much she really affects you. Guard your heart at all costs.

He remembered stories of his grandfather's days. He admitted to one of his wives that he couldn't help himself from falling in love with her. That she did something to him to make him want to do anything for her. To make her happy. To please her.

He had told her he simply couldn't live without her.

Well, she really took it to town. She manipulated the hell out of him. She was secretly involved with one of his competitors. She would finagle money and other valuables out of him. Using excuses that if she didn't get it, she'd leave him, she'd be devastated, she would shrivel up and die. Pouted when she didn't get her way. Used the kids as bait, leverage, an excuse.

She drained the poor man. Of his pride. His finances. And eventually, his life. He loved her so passionately and believed in her so vehemently, that when she did up and leave him after all that, he fell real hard.

Stop it, Evan. This is not that old floozy. This is sweet, honest, reliable Emma Wiggins.

Still, his grandfather, his uncles, his own father believed in the women they fell for—then fell hard for. His old man always told him to "have a relationship, if you will—but never fall in love."

Well, he couldn't possibly have a relationship with Emma Wiggins because he was falling totally, irrevocably, undeniably in love with her. Every inch of her. Inside and out.

"What do I do to you?" Emma's voice was soft and sensual. She leaned in closer to him. He was still stiff below.

She reached up and placed her arms around the back of his neck. She kissed him gently. Her lips brushing against his. Seductive and warm as molasses. The heat was climbing in the hotel room. The heat between them.

His heartbeat quickened. He returned the favor and devoured her lips. He knew he would probably regret this later.

But he loved her.
He wanted her.
He wanted her…Now.

Emma could not believe this was happening. Only in her most lascivious dreams. Evan Fletcher was kissing her. His soft lips travelled all over her body.

She was locked in his sweet embrace. She didn't remember when her attire came off, but before long, they were both naked. On the bed. He had pulled out a condom before they undressed. The plush hotel room was dimly lit. The satin covers of the bed encased them as they were enrapt between the sheets. He kissed her gently from her forehead, to her nose to her lips, her neck and her bosoms. She addressed his firm, muscular flesh with the same.

Gosh, he had rock hard abs. He certainly was buff from head to toe. She shivered with every touch of his body, with every warm, sultry embrace. Excitement increased within her as he eased into her, capturing the moment.

She tingled from head to toe. *Ohmygod! He really knows how to make love*, Emma mused with delight. She didn't remember when the last time she'd done this.

She'd only had one relationship prior, not something she ever wanted anyone to know about, feeling like such a sheltered wallflower—and that was hardly anything compared to this. In fact, it was nothing compared to this moment. This was love. She was in love with Evan. Everything about him.

She'd almost wished that this was her first time. It sure felt like it was. Her heartbeat quickened with every breathy movement.

Suddenly, all the cares of the world melted away with his warmth, his gentleness, his caress. Every concern evaporated.

She felt so on top of the world.

So special.

So loved.

So cared for.

They made hot, passionate, scream-out-loud love on the warm, breezy New York City night.

"God, I love you, Emma. I love you so much. You have no idea." Evan's deep voice was throaty, husky, breathless as he continued to make love to her.

She moaned with pleasure, "Love you, too, baby."

There was no doubt about it. They were both in denial about their feelings for each other prior to this. Evan was relieved Emma felt the same way he did.

All too soon it was early the next morning in Emma's hotel room. Their flight would leave later that day. Evan rolled over with a wide grin and mellow eyes. He so badly wanted to hug Emma.

She was gone.

Where had she gone? Evan was bewildered. His stomach tightened and it had nothing to do with how he usually felt after a good workout of his abs.

A thought gripped him.

Did she have a change of heart over last night? Did she have any regrets? He knew that he sure didn't. He enjoyed every last moment of his passion with Emma. In fact, he'd never felt that way about any of the women he'd ever dated.

How sad was that?

He pulled back the soft duvet and sprung up out of bed. Just then, he heard the door open.

Emma walked in with a take-out bag from the restaurant downstairs and two coffees.

She froze.

Emma couldn't believe Evan stood naked right in front of her. She'd never seen such a full view of his body like this before. She flushed. She felt hot inside.

He was certainly blessed with a good, strong, hot body. She tried not to gape at his midsection. She almost dropped the drink tray with the two coffees.

"Here, let me take that," he offered as he walked close to her. She felt giddy. Okay, she'd always dreamed of seeing him naked, imagined what he'd be like. Now she knew. Full well. She chuckled sheepishly.

"Thanks, I thought I'd grab us something to eat. You know, room service is so crazy expensive."

A puzzled expression made its way on his face then vanished quickly. "Hey, you know I've got it covered." He grinned.

She hoped he didn't take it the wrong way.

The truth was, she really needed to get some air. Clear her mind. Rejuvenate her thoughts. She'd just had the best time of her life—as far as she could remember off the top of her head. So why did something feel off—so wrong?

A good, brisk early morning walk in the heart of New York seemed like the fitting thing to do.

She took in the sights of the city, the sound of traffic moving, honking of horns, witnessed business people scurrying to work, tourists getting an early start to the day. The sunshine was bright in the morning. She walked through the ever-so-busy-never-a-dull-moment Times Square and saw many pedestrians sitting, walking, or parking themselves each seemingly with a good book to read. In fact, a lot of people just sort of settled themselves there since they closed off some of the roads to traffic and relaxed or met up with friends. It was quite special to see.

Emma made her way over to a park nearby and sat on a park bench looking up at the sky and watching the wind rustle the tree leaves on the branches. Enjoying the scenery. Enjoying nature in the middle of the concrete jungle.

She even watched as the water flowed from the crystal blue water fountain. It looked breathtaking. Beautiful.

For some strange reason, the endless flow reminded her of the legendary fountain of youth-often referred to as the water of life. Her grandfather used to tell her stories about the fountain of youth that could apparently restore the youth of anyone who drank from its spring waters. The tales, from over one thousand years ago, have stretched from the Caribbean to Africa to Europe.

She had a moment of sorrow touch her heart. She wished of all wishes, that it was somehow real. She'd walk over to the fountain and take some in a bottle to bring to her grandfather. She really couldn't bear the thought of losing him. Ever. It gripped her heart and squeezed it to think of such a thing.

She decided to give him a call on her BlackBerry as she sat on the park bench. Her trench coat folded over her. She searched in her purse and pulled out the phone and powered it on.

When Gramps answered, he was in a cheery mood, but the nurse was also there about to give him his daily injection. She didn't want to disturb and told him she'd see him very soon. She just couldn't wait to be near him again.

"Love you, too, pumpkin," he said in a groggy, morning voice.

"Love you more, Gramps," she replied, melting at the sound of his voice. She really did miss him.

"Can't wait to see you married next week."

Oops!

She felt heat rush from her again. Drained clear out of her face. She'd almost forgotten about her promise to him. This was ironic because she just made love last night to her groom-to-be. Which happened to be her boss. Something that made her stomach clench.

What was she thinking? How could she face him at the office, like nothing happened?

What will their behavior towards each other be like at the office? Would this affect her work? Evan's work? What if everyone at the office found out?

"Are you two having a good time?"

"Yes, Gramps. Everything is great." Well, that wasn't quite a lie. They spent a passionate night together. People who are engaged do those things, you know.

"Gramps?"

"Yes, dear."

"You called the office yesterday."

"Yes, dear."

"Is everything alright?"

"Oh, pumpkin," he gave a hearty chuckled then coughed as if he had choked on his own saliva.

"Gramps, you okay?" Panic rose in her chest.

"Yes, pumpkin. I just got a little tickle in my throat."

"Oh dear, is the nurse still there?"

"Yes, pumpkin. She's giving me a bed bath now."

"Okay, I don't want to disturb your morning routine." Emma bit down on her lip and asked to speak briefly to the nurse to make sure everything was alright. She was about to ask her grandfather what exactly he said to the receptionist when he called but didn't want to risk troubling his mind. After all, he had bigger things to worry about and it wasn't quite his fault she'd led him to believe that she was engaged to Evan Fletcher.

When she got back to the hotel, she decided to stop by the café on the ground floor of the restaurant to grab a quick bite and a cup of coffee. She figured, why not get something for Evan, too?

She clarified what she meant by picking up breakfast for Evan and herself and they both proceeded to pack to and get ready to head over to the airport.

Evan had spoken to their client beforehand and made other arrangements. He went over to the office to do last minute consults. He was in awe of the photos from the shoot the day prior. He began to twitch again. The feeling was more pleasant than he cared to admit. Another thought dawned in his head. How were they going to act at the office? With what they'd just been through? He knew it was probably not the best of decisions to make love when out of town on a client shoot. What if she became clingy? Needy? What if she wanted more from him? More from their business relationship? Where would this leave him? And his company he'd worked so hard to build—the right way. Most importantly, where would this leave Emma? She was the last person on this planet he wanted to hurt in any way, shape, or form.

Speaking of forms.

He glanced back to the photo spread on the boardroom table of the client's office. Emma was stunning. He couldn't believe how beautiful she was and how he would marry her next week in a fake wedding ceremony. Still, it was for the best that it was only pretend.

Damn that Fletcher curse!

13

"So, how was New York?" Lucinda narrowed her green eyes as Emma strolled through the glass doors of Fletcher Advertising on Monday morning.

She noticed Lucinda's facial expression seemed to betray her overly-cheerful, try-too-hard tone. Lucinda's auburn hair seemed to gleam with the early morning sun blazing through the tall windows of the reception area. Kiku, a plump woman from accounting, stood at the reception desk facing Lucinda. It appeared as if they had been engaged in a very private conversation before Emma walked in. Kiku was here early, Emma observed.

Kiku turned around and forced a polite smile to Emma. "Yes, how was New York?" Kiku chimed in.

"It was good. We got a lot accomplished," Emma offered. She then paused in front of the reception desk after her legs transported her from the entrance doors towards Lucinda's desk. Her three-quarter length spring trench coat hung open in a stylish way. In addition, she had her briefcase in one hand, Gucci-imitation bag swung over her left shoulder—her shades placed above her head.

Kiku then turned her attention back to Lucinda. Emma could not hear exactly what words were exchanged, but by the low whispers and mumbles under the breath, she'd bet it wasn't nice—in fact, she thought she heard one of them mumble "I'll bet it was" under her gossip-toned breath followed by a sly giggle. But she let it slide—just like water off a duck's back. She was far too above the influence of the O.P. (office politics) drug. Good thing after being shuffled around as a kid, she developed leather-thick skin and a focused mind.

Gramps always said that if people are talking behind your back, then you're probably walking in the right direction. Still, when people—especially those with whom you work—said nasty things behind your back or to your side, it stung. Like an insect bite. You don't know quite when it bit, or how it bit, or what the side-effects would be, but it was annoying as hell.

Emma smiled confidently, not afraid to nip it in the bud. "Hey, what's funny?" she asked cheerfully, as she pulled her coat off and slung it over her arm. She leaned on the high reception glass round desk with her bags in her hands. Waiting.

Lucinda and Kiku froze.

"Oh, nothing," Lucinda sputtered with hesitation caught in her throat. Gosh, that deer-caught-in-the-headlights look was hilarious on Lucinda.

Emma smiled and shook her head as she muscled up her bags and headed towards her office. "Have a nice day, ladies." Emma was off. It was as if nothing bothered her. And why should it? She knew that gossip may surface if Gramps mentioned anything about the wedding fiancé thing between her and Evan. She could just see the headlines now on the old office gossip grapevine: Receptionist promoted to account coordinator then executive overnight via horizontal promotion.

Emma rolled her eyes at the mere thought of it. Gossip was nothing more than a verbally transmitted disease, according to Gramps, that attacks thoughts, ruins lives, and cripples reputations.

Still she was going to prove herself immune from Lucinda's vocal venom. Gramps always told her: "You have to know which battles to fight and which to walk away from." She loved her Gramps.

A crippling pain shot up in her belly when she thought she could lose him any day. He always told her she was destined for great stuff and to not let little annoyances of life throw her off balance or derail her from her true purpose and mission in life.

Emma moved up the glass spiral steps to the second level of the loft towards her office. She could see through her blind spot that the girls still were frozen at reception—gaping up at her as she made her way up the steps, with defined footsteps of her heels. She shrugged if off—mentally. She really wasn't about to let other opinions bother her.

Not now.

Not ever.

Truth be told, between her beloved Gramps dying and her upcoming wedding—she had bigger issues bubbling up her pot right now.

And speaking of weddings, Emma glanced towards Evan's office on the way to her own office, but was sadly disappointed—no, peeved. She was definitely peeved that he wasn't in his office or at his desk. Evan would usually be the first on the work scene—a workaholic trait of his she had warned him about playfully.

She swallowed.

She reached into her handbag once she got into her office and then closed the door behind her. She pulled out her BlackBerry and firmly pressed the number keys.

The sound of Evan's deep, silky voice boomed through the speaker of her cell phone.

"Hi, you've reached 555-1218, please leave a message and I'll get back to you as soon as possible." Beep!

Emma already left a message for Evan this weekend. She loved to hear his voice but not by way of a recording. She hung up immediately.

"What's going on?"

Ever since they landed back in Texas, Evan had been—what's the word?

Standoffish.

He hadn't returned her phone calls over the weekend, which Emma thought was strangely peculiar. She didn't want to appear the needy, Velcro-clingy type— the stuff she'd once overheard him talking about in terms of what turns him off a woman.

Still, the man owed her a phone call. They had the most intimate night together brimming with hot, intense passion. Was she just a past time fling to him? A fun way to kill time in the Big Apple? She shuddered at the thought.

Emma felt the heat rise in her chest like a volcano about to erupt. Then the inferno promptly travelled towards her cheek the moved its way up to her temples. She got up from her seat and closed the window blinds of her glass office so that nobody else in the loft could see her. She sat back down at her desk, logged on the computer, placed her elbows on the desk, and began massaging her temples. Her eyes closed tightly.

Breathe in-2-3-4.

Breathe out 2-3-4.

She practiced. She just had to get a solid grip on herself before she lost her mind over Evan. But he sure was stirring her crazy. Not just stirring in the common sense. He was spinning her mind into a cocktail of confusion. How could she have read into what happened in New York so wrong? That's what you get for sleeping with the boss, girl.

Stupid.

Stupid.

Stupid.

"Evan, where are you?"

Just then, another thought spun into her mind like a Texas high wind. What if he was hurt? What if something bad happened to him? She sat back down to use the phone.

Oh. My. God.

She immediately picked up the silver receiver of her high-tech executive phone then slammed it back down into its cradle.

She dropped the phone receiver as if it were a hot piece of coal. She was about to call Lucinda at reception to ask if she'd seen or heard from Evan.

Emma got up again and paced with her arms folded across her chest.

What to do? Oh, what to do?

Emma raked her fingers through her thick, lustrous, springy curls, then paused to give her conundrum some thought. The action of moving through her hair just reminded her of Evan's gentle touch as he explored her locks during their warm embrace. He admired her natural curls, she could tell. She squeezed her eyes shut then opened them again.

Think straight, she scolded herself.

"Oh, dear God." She clasped her hand over her forehead, paced again, and stopped. "Here I was thinking Evan was dodging me when he could be—missing!"

She picked up the phone receiver once again. To hell with what Lucinda thinks, she challenged. I need to know if anyone's heard from Evan. At all. I need to know if he's alright.

"Yes?" Lucinda picked up the phone rather abruptly from the reception desk. If Emma were to crack open her blinds and peek over, she could get a good view of the reception area from her office in the open concept design of the agency. But she dared not. It sounded as if she had bothered Lucinda from something critically important.

Still, manners should never go AWOL when you're the corporation's first impression. Though Lucinda could see on her call display phone the numbers of external numbers and the names of employees that flash across the phone's high-tech screen for internal calls, she should never forget the art of politeness. Coworker or client, all should be addressed with utmost respect.

Perhaps Emma's mindset was different since she had been raised—though by her grandparents—from a very old-school way of doing things.

Did Lucinda have something against Emma because they both started out as receptionists at the ad agency? What was ironic was that Emma had been the one to encourage Lucinda to take the college courses in advertising and business with her at the local college to upgrade in the advertising industry. They both had agreed that it was an exciting field. Both agreed to sign up. But Lucinda never bothered and said she didn't have the time and was happy being reception. Emma shrugged it off at the time. She would speak to Lucinda at another time.

"Lucinda, has Evan called in?" Emma couldn't wait to let the words roll off her tongue. With equal anticipation, she couldn't wait to hear the answer. Her heartbeat accelerated in her chest.

Silence.

Emma could hear Lucinda smacking her gum into the phone. Was she enjoying this? Honestly, she was going to sit down and chat with Lucinda on her phone manners—still, Emma waited.

"Nope!" Lucinda continued to chew gum audibly.

"No?" Alarm rose in Emma's voice. She didn't want to be the one to raise any suspicion or unnecessary panic. Lord knows she had enough supply within to be spooning it out to everybody else. Still, she was all too familiar that gossip travelled quicker than the speed of e-mail in the office.

One false word and that was it!

Still, as Gramps once told her in a famous quote: Bright people talk about ideas. Average people talk about things. And small people talk about other people.

Right now, Emma didn't care how she would look to small-minded people.

"Well, that's strange. He's usually here first thing Monday morning, bright and early. We have the weekly meeting soon."

More silence.

More silence followed by that annoying gum-smacking Olympics Lucinda had going on in her mouth. Emma wanted to shout out, "Will you just stop it, already!?"

"You know, you really shouldn't be chewing gum while talking on the phone," she wanted to say. But she'd never seen Lucinda being overtly rude in the presence of clients, admittedly. Not as far as she knew. And quite frankly, she wasn't about to hand over the extra satisfaction to let Lucinda know it bothered her.

"Oh, wait a minute. Hold on," Lucinda said. Emma could hear Lucinda tapping into her keyboard. The soft sounds of the keys. As receptionist, Lucinda often checked her e-mails first thing in the morning. Emma figured she must have just gotten more e-mails.

"Well, well, well," Lucinda chimed. She then murmured bits of the e-mail as she read it under her breath. "Yep. Seems like he left a message he'd be back in the office on Tuesday."

"What?" Heat climbed in Emma's throat. Why didn't he tell Emma about this? And why didn't she get the e-mail, too, on her BlackBerry?

Emma thanked Lucinda then hung up the phone. What was Evan playing at now? Was he trying to show her something? Emma logged onto her desktop computer and tapped her fingernails on her desk as she waited for the Fletcher Advertising logo to launch, then…

She logged onto her internal e-mail and waited briefly for the inbox to spring up. One of the downsides to being out of the office for a few good days was the amount of new e-mails piled up in the inbox. Of course, she only connected her personal e-mail accounts to her BlackBerry phone.

"You have 175 unread messages."

"Great." She sighed and clicked on the inbox logo. Most of the e-mails were impersonal ones from suppliers and associates, some spam and other nuisance correspondence.

None of the e-mails were from Evan.

Crap.

She clicked out on the logout button on the top of the screen and swung her chair away from the desk and leaned back.

Okay, so he's not hurt. He's just "not that into me," she mused in relation to a popular book she had read.

The ringing sound of the phone distracted Emma's pity party. She reached quickly to pick it up. It had to be Evan.

"Hey, girl, it's me Genie."

"Oh." Oops, she sounded a bit too disappointed. She quickly acted to uplift her tone but Genie already slipped some more of her own words in.

"Sorry, were you expecting someone else? Oh, let me guess—Evan still hasn't called you back."

"Yep." She sighed heavily. "Still no answer."

"Is he alright?" Genie sounded alarmed, concerned.

"Oh, yeah," Emma sighed, nonchalantly. "Lucinda informed me that he sent her an e-mail this morning. But none to me, of course. I don't know what's gotten into him. Maybe he thinks I'm-"

"No. Don't even say it, girl. You are the last person in the world who is easy. It's not like you haven't spent a lot of time with him in the past. Not like you ever flirted with him before when you did have a chance. You both were caught up in the moment of passion—that happens, girlfriend. And besides, you're both getting married this week. For better or for worse."

Emma swallowed. "Oh, yeah. That's another thing. I'm just wondering if he's had a change of heart or cold feet or worse."

"Didn't he tell you he was going to go along with it?"

"Yes, but—"

"But nothing, girl. Just don't take things too hard. I'm sure there's a perfectly good reason why he hasn't called you back yet."

"Oh, yeah. And I just can't wait to hear it."

Before getting off the phone, Genie reminded Emma that she had to go to the Bridal Boutique to pick out the simple dress she had tried on once. For the ceremony, of course. Emma was debating whether she should rent it or buy it for the day.

She had already spoken to the woman at the boutique who agreed that she could make any rush adjustments within twenty-four hours for Emma.

Emma hoped it wouldn't take too long since she wanted to swing by the hospital again. She spent most of the weekend with Gramps, pushing him around in his wheelchair on the hospital grounds, the garden, the park. She took him to a nice themed park where they had a barbecue. Gramps enjoyed the fiasco. She really wanted to make it up to him for not being there with him during the few days she had to be in New York. It would have been nice if Evan could have been there. Gramps asked several times about Evan.

Emma swallowed hard.

Still, she had promised Gramps he would meet Evan soon. She only wished and hoped in her heart that Evan would not let her down. But then, he wasn't usually the type to. And he was working closely with her on this new Weddings R Us account. Why would he want to risk ruining their personal relationship?

Emma had visited Gramps on her way to work, too. He chastised her for coming in too much. "Pumpkin, you're gonna wear yourself down. I don't want you getting all burned out on my account."

"Oh, Gramps! There's no such thing as me getting burned out—certainly not on your account. Trust me, this is a picnic. A walk in the park for me."

Really, it was.

Emma thought of the countless times Gramps had been there for her when she was growing up and going through her most difficult times.

The sacrifices he'd made to go to her art classes, her recitals, her games. He worked hard all day and took time off whenever it had anything to do with his granddaughter.

He missed out on some of his beloved bridge games to make her events if he had to. How could she not return the favor? How could she not want to return the favor? She enjoyed his company and would miss him terribly when he departed. She really wanted to spend as much of her time with him as she could.

Besides, she wanted to ensure that he got proper care and wasn't neglected because of short staffing at the facility. She wanted to sit with him and feed him. To help him. The nurses did an excellent job but with one nurse to ten patients, it seemed as though someone could get short changed. The nurse may be a wonder-person, but certainly could not attend so many patients effectively. They couldn't possibly be in ten or twenty rooms—all at the same time.

That was simply impossible.

She worried because Gramps was too shy to press the nurse call button because he didn't like to "bother anyone." Trouble was, Emma watched for herself how the nurse kept coming into his room and asking if he needed anything to which he would always say he's good.

Then he may or may not hesitate before spurting out, "Well actually, I wouldn't mind another glass of juice, if you don't mind."

The nurse would then smile and get it for him right away. Still, Gramps said he felt bad to have to trouble people for things he used to be able to do himself.

Emma reminded him that he once used to get things for people, including a roof over the head of his family and food in their bellies and much more so there was certainly nothing wrong with having the favour returned now that he really needed the help and be on the receiving end.

"It's called turn taking, Gramps," Emma had said as she smiled and gave his shoulders a good squeeze.

After she got off the phone with Genie once they'd made arrangements to meet for lunch, Emma turned back to the computer screen. With her mouse, she clicked on the Weddings R Us folder and proceeded to do last minute touches on designing their new company logo they had agreed for her to work on.

A few hours breezed by quickly. Emma glanced at the clock on the computer and couldn't believe it was already lunchtime. She had been so absorbed in working on the Weddings R Us logo design, back and forth on the phone with the client in New York, finishing up on other projects she had for other clients and so forth.

Emma was glad the sun shined bright as she glanced over at her office window. The scenery was beautiful. She enjoyed her loft glass office. She was grateful Evan took his employees' environment into consideration. Not only did everyone have ergonomically friendly furniture, but their equipment was high tech with the best of options.

He always told his employees that a relaxed mind is a creative mind. He also made it a point that everyone should have a good view of the lake and the beautiful scenery of Mercy Springs. That was why he chose that office space on the top level of the four-story glass building.

Also, he felt that a beautiful environment sparked creativity. So if you were on the top floor of the loft, so much the better. Not that accounting didn't have a good view. He studied the psychology of colors and took great care in designing the office space from the beginning. He certainly worked hard and paid attention to the minute details. Emma bit down on her lip. She hoped he hadn't forgotten the little detail about a getting married to her this week.

Later, she crossed over the street to the Bridal Boutique. At least something was shining bright in her life at the moment—the warmth of the sun mellowed her skin. The right amount of cool breeze calmed her.

She didn't want to push the whole Evan thing right now. She was planning on discussing their arrangement with him tomorrow—and a few other things, too. She really didn't want him to think she was incapable without his presence. They'd made an agreement. He was a man of his word. That was that. She'd at least give him a chance before ringing off his ear.

When she saw the Mercy Springs Bridal Boutique sign, Emma thought back to her trip to New York and her most recent client. She would just love to use their services. But it wouldn't be right. It certainly wouldn't be professional. Especially given the fact that she was pretending to marry the boss. She shook her head and grinned—she could just see the look on Ms. Endo's face if she ever found out the truth. She would just have a huge hissy fit. She would probably chastise Emma about using the institution—the sacred institution of marriage for personal gain.

The door chime sounded as Emma walked in the boutique. She spun around when the attendant approached her.

"Welcome back, stranger." The woman held out her hand and shook Emma's.

"Thanks for seeing me on such short notice. I just got back from New York."

"No probs. Let's get going. You said you were meeting a friend here?"

Just then, the door chime sounded again and Genie waltz through with her school bag swung over her back, her shades on and jeans with a spring jacket.

"Sorry I'm late," Genie said as she walked up on the hardwood floor, her black, leather ankle boots stomping hard on the wood, making a clopping sound. She looked so cool, so relaxed. Emma was thankful she could make it in between her classes. Talk about a caring friend. Loyal, more like it. She may not have much family, but even if she could count one friend on her hand—that would be enough.

"I was just getting things together." The woman went around the corner then came back with a gown in her hand. She held it carefully, like a delicate piece of art.

"You know, on average, a bride usually has three dress fittings—"

"Told you," Genie interrupted the bridal shop attendant as she raised a brow to Emma.

The shop attendant didn't seem too impressed with the bordering-on-rude outburst. She cleared her throat, then continued. "As I was saying, a bride usually has three dress fittings. The first involves major alterations. The very last fitting would be taking care of all the fine details." The attendant placed the gown on the table.

"I know you had your eye on this one last week, when you came in here in that panic rush. I'll make an exception in your case, since you want to speed things up with your grandfather's condition." The bridal attendant clasped her hands to her chest and smiled as she tilted her head staring off into space. "How sweet. That is so romantic. I hope my grandkids don't forget me when they're getting married. Especially if I end up in the situation like your dear grandfather. How old is he again?"

Emma swallowed. "He's eighty. He's going to be…" Emma broke off, almost in tears. The words got caught in her throat momentarily. She wanted to say that he'll be eighty-one on Christmas Day but the truth was, according to what the doctors told her, he wouldn't be around Christmas Day. She fanned herself inside and tried to push those thoughts away. That was just too overwhelming for her.

Sensing her discomfort, Genie reached over and squeezed Emma's shoulder. Where would she be without supportive friends like Genie?

"Well, let's get going then, shall we?" The bridal attendant explained to Emma that she would get all the finishing touches done pronto. Of course, Emma was spending a hefty amount for her appreciation of their rush efforts.

She stood on the stool and had the dress placed over her. She remembered what the lady had said about undergarments being left with the gown. She pulled out of her bag her silk lingerie that she would be wearing under the dress.

"Good. Good," the bridal attendant said as she proceeded to pin the parts of the dress that were too big for Emma. "I'll take those from you later. It's imperative we have everything you'll be wearing for the day and that will go with the dress. I can't stress this enough," the woman said with pins in her mouth sticking out as she removed each one by one to pin to the appropriate areas. She stood back and looked at Emma as if eyeing a model on a runway. She tilted her head to see if it fitted the way it should.

Emma gushed at her friend Genie who was busy grinning and shaking her head, all the while making small talk to settle her nerves. Genie was one of the most honest people she'd ever known. She really wanted and got her opinion about everything. A feat to which Emma was truly grateful. Emma could not believe she was actually going through with this.

It all seemed so—surreal.

Emma had dreamed about this day. To be a bride. To be fitted. Of course, this whole getting married this week was a bit unexpected. She smiled to herself. She was glad to be doing this for Gramps.

Emma had her bodice fitted. The attendant checked her for comfort and accuracy. And told Emma to walk around with all the adjustments to see if she was comfortable.

"You know," the woman warned her, "bridal gowns have a nasty habit of behaving differently on the day of the wedding when they are finally stitched. I know you're pressed for time, but after I make the adjustments, I'll need you to come back and you can do the walk all over again."

Truth be told, it was a small wedding ceremony. Micro. But she wanted to do this thing right. After all, it may just be the closest thing to walking down the aisle Emma would ever have.

She swallowed. A sigh followed.

Gosh, she'd longed for a happy, normal—whatever normal was—slice of life, love, and happiness. She longed to have what she did not—could not have. A happy home, marriage, a tiny dog, children, a husband who adored her, a family life she cherished.

Instead, here she was—an unexpected bride.

An unexpected bride who was partly deceiving the groom-to-be to marry her for real so that her grandfather wouldn't go to his grave depressed thinking that the only heir to his bloodline may very well end up dead, destitute, and alone—with maybe a cat.

Emma walked around the elaborate boutique. It was so hard not to be absorbed into the whole wedding spirit. She'd really wished Evan were there. Her Gramps, too. And, her mother. Maybe the Evan part wouldn't be such a good idea, since he shouldn't see Emma in her bridal gown before the wedding.

The store was beautiful. The dim lights created an intimate, relaxed, cosy ambiance. There were rows of different colored dresses for the bridal party. A mannequin of the bride and groom were dressed appropriately. A comfortable cream coloured sofa sat off to the side so guests and friends of the bride could make themselves at home.

Rows of shoes on a rack caused Genie and Emma both to gush over all the choices earlier. And golden colored dressing rooms with gold satin curtains and a large full mirror offered perfect refuge for trying on everything and anything. Emma saw mother-of-the-bride dresses to which made her belly tighten. She longed to have her mother in her life. She wished this were for real. She hoped she and her mother could be closer. But even after the wedding, what would her mother think if she suddenly upped and got an annulment—after Gramps passed. She cringed at the thought and reshifted her focus.

There were prom gowns and many synthetic bouquets, apparently handcrafted. Emma's eyes froze when she got a good look at the bouquet held by the female bridal mannequin. It was a bouquet alright.

And not just any bouquet either.

It was a beautiful bouquet woven from phalaenopsis orchids trimmed with stephanotis and the whole thing flowed to the ground.

It was breathtaking.

She knew it was supposed to be a small ceremony, but she would love to have that arrangement.

Genie immediately followed her friend's gaze to the object of her salivation. She eyed the elaborate bouquet carried in the slender plastic fingers of the mannequin bride.

"Oh. No," Genie shook her head and emphasized hand gestures signifying when a director yells cut.

"Oh. Yes," Emma answered back.

The seamstress, who was altering Emma's dress, looked from Emma to Genie and back again. She grinned and continued to put last minute touches on the dress.

Emma simply fell in love with the floral arrangement. Its beautiful petals and elegant appearance seemed to call to her.

And much like happiness in her life, she had to have it.

After the dress fitting, Emma returned the favor and assisted Genie, the only girl in her bridal party, with her bridesmaid dress.

It was a soft peach-coloured satin dress that flowed to the ankles.

It was beautiful.

Emma thought the dress would be perfect for Genie. Besides, much like her gown, those dresses could easily be worn at a fancy dinner party or other formal event. The thing she loved about the boutique dresses was they were versatile.

Emma was deeply appreciative of Genie going along with this—though part of her pained to think it wasn't real. There was still that little psychosomatic nudging in the pit of her belly.

She really wanted it to seem as real as possible. For Gramps's sake, especially. Still, what was she thinking? she mused. Evan still hadn't spoken to her since they returned from New York. But that was fine. The show would go on.

Evan was a man of honor. He would do the right thing.

Emma had no doubt as to his integrity.

"Okay, kiddo, now back to you." Genie undressed out of her gown in the changing room. Her dress seemed to fit her perfectly with little alteration needed.

"Back to me?"

"Yep. You know the drill. If we're gonna do this, we're gonna do it right. Now…" She paused and put her hand on her chin and crossed her other arm across her chest when she dressed back into her day clothes.

"Something blue. You can borrow my pearl bracelet my grandmother gave to me."

"Aw. Thanks so much, Genie."

Emma's eyes misted over. Not just because of Genie's warm offer but also because she was reminded of her own grandmother who had passed away. When she told Gramps she was getting married, he asked to see his valuables in the safe. He then immediately gave Emma his late wife's—Emma's grandmother's—beautiful pearl necklace she wore when they got married.

This touched Emma deeply in the very core of her soul. How could she even begin to think of letting him down? He had told her that he never thought he would live to see the day when he could give it to Emma—with her being single for so long with no prospects in sight. But that was the greatest day of his life, he told her, and it showed.

The moment where he could pass on one of the finest Wiggins family treasures. Emma told him, of course, that he and Grandma were the Wiggins finest treasure.

They both had a tear-jerking moment when they reminisced about Grandma and her wonderful old-fashioned loving ways. Emma missed her terribly, just as she knew she would miss Gramps like crazy.

"So something old…" Genie interrupted her mindful walk down memory lane.

"Something new!" Emma chimed in.

"Something borrowed."

"And something blue." Both girls laughed out loud, hugged and squeezed each other like sisters. This was certainly a moment to remember.

"You know, doll, life is about moments, isn't it?"

"Sure got that right. We have to make each moment a special occasion as Gramps would drill in my head every single day."

"Yep. Quit worrying about the future or if things will work out. That's a first class ticket to Ulcer City."

Emma giggled. Genie really knew how to make light a situation. Gosh, just think if she had gone on her own to do the bridal fitting.

Emma turned the key to her apartment and let herself in. It had been a crazy long day at work when she got back to the office after the bridal dress fitting. Still, she felt as if she moved a huge step further with the plan. Even though there was already a glitch to her almost perfect day.

Still no word from Evan.

The groom-to-be.

She spun by the hospital to see her Gramps and help him with his dinner tray, but not because she felt the nurses wouldn't help him. But in his last days, she really wanted to make sure he was not alone. She was happy to spend time with him. The thought of him being alone terrified her. It kept her awake at nights.

Then she thought to herself, What if Gramps didn't have her?

Who would visit him morning, day, and night? Who would call him around the clock and sit in meetings with doctors and nurses and the social work team regarding his plan of care?

She tried to gently push the negative what-ifs out of her head. Gramps always told her that what-ifs are one of the greatest ulcer-inducing habits known to man. Especially when people had a bad, obsessive, life-crippling case of it.

She smiled to herself as she placed her keys on the side table by the entrance of her apartment door. She really was going to miss Gramps's little philosophies.

Would she have grandkids one day to be able to share her own life's wisdom with? She hoped her story would travel in that direction. She so wanted a family—a husband and children, at least one, anyway—of her own to love, honour, cherish, and enjoy.

She instinctively switched on the TV with the remote control before pulling off her coat to see if she could catch any interesting news on the twenty-four hour news station. She walked into the kitchen and turned on the kettle to make her usual cup of green tea.

She was still full after the scrumptious lunch she had with Genie after the bridal dress fitting. Emma laughed at the sight when they were done.

Their bellies had swelled from all that delicious food they started to thank their lucky stars they hadn't eaten before the bridal dress fitting. That reminded her she'd better not over-stuff herself before walking down that aisle.

SHADONNA RICHARDS

Because of Emma's hard work and serious
overtime in landing the new account, Evan had already
agreed that all those who worked on the case could take an
extra long lunch hour or leave early for the afternoon.

Evan had gone as far as to give a day off in lieu of
overtime. But Emma decided to hold off on that for now.
Until a long weekend cropped up. She would use her time
then to take an extra-long weekend break. It felt like a
mini vacation then.

As she flipped through the different news stations
with her satellite channels, Emma sighed.

Nothing out of the ordinary.

A star athlete caught in a media-frenzy sex
scandal. A politician with a skeleton that accidently
stormed out of his closet right after he announced his
intention to run for office. A love-child with a secret
mistress sort of popped out of nowhere.

Emma shook her head and sighed.

She heard the kettle click off. She sprung up from
microsuede sofa and back into the kitchen to fix her cup of
tea. She loved it steaming hot with a teaspoon of warm
honey and, of course, no milk. It was delicious. Once
she'd heard the main headlines, scandals, and bad news,
she went into the bathroom to run the bath. She was going
to soak in the tub with her green tea and a good book to
read. Her only company right now.

As Emma ran the water, she heard the loud
knocking on the door. Who could it be? Evan? Her heart
leapt. She sprung up on her feet and went to answer the
door.

She squinted through the peep hole but could not
in a million years believe her eyes.

"No. Way!"

When the door opened wide, Emma's shock
expanded at the vision in front of her.

14

"Mom?" Emma's voice was a pitch higher than usual. She stood there frozen.

"Well, are you gonna let me in—or are we gonna have our little heart to heart out here in the hallway so the neighbours can listen in?"

Emma swallowed.

She had a mixture of emotions stirring inside. Shock was one of them. But once she unfroze herself, she immediately snapped back into normalcy. She clapped her hand to her forehead. "Of course, Mom." She stepped back apologetically, with an air of embarrassment.

Stupid.

Stupid.

Stupid.

She just hadn't expected her mother to be here so soon. But then again, why was she so surprised? Her wedding was this week.

Ms. Wiggins kept her married name though she had divorced from Emma's father a long time ago. She figured it would be easier than changing all of her ID—again.

She'd accomplished a lot, including earning a college degree while married to Emma's father. She wore a green jacket with a large round hat, red handbag, and leopard skin tights with stiletto heels. Ms. Wiggins certainly was a fun, eclectic type.

Still, Emma and her mother were as different as lion and lamb. She was more of stranger than anything else, Emma was sad to admit. She longed to call her Mommy. To have that normal mother-daughter thing going on. But still, she had her Gramps and Grandma who made up for it big time. She figured her mother got thrown into the marriage game a little too early for her personal life and it came too sudden. She wasn't terribly maternal—as some mothers would be. But Emma tried to focus on her individuality and her good points. We're not all cut out from the same mould, Gramps would stress.

Ms. Wiggins gawked as if she were in a museum as she took in the sight of her daughter's apartment. The African artwork on the wall and a large ornament from the Orient caught her eye. There was a mixture of art from different parts of the world. It was her first visit to her daughter's home in Texas. She was ashamed it took so long.

Ms. Wiggins clutched tightly to her handbag as if in a tourist resort and didn't want to let go for fear of being mugged. You would think she was at a stranger's house and not her offspring's home.

"Fiancé having a bath?" she commented, hearing the water running in the bathroom. She stretched her long, slender neck around the corner to see if she could see anything.

"Huh?" Emma took a moment before she realised what her mother was saying. "Oh. No…" She shook her head and chuckled.

Oops!

She was about to let pose: Why would I be living with Evan? But that would just sound so stupid. Almost as inane as saying why would the sky be blue?

"Um. Well…actually, Mom, he's not here."

"No?" Her mother seemed appalled. Almost stunned.

"Good heavens, why not? Where is he? Working late at the office?"

"Well. No. Not exactly." Emma felt as if she were a witness in a high profile case and she was being interrogated by the star prosecutor—an intimidating experience.

"What do you mean, not exactly?" Her mother narrowed her eyes. She spun her head around and did a quick scan of the apartment. "Does a man even live here? Where are his things?"

Ms. Wiggins quickly poked her head into the closet and looked at the shoe rack by the door.

All women's shoes.

She helped herself to a quick tour.

Not that Emma wasn't going to offer her a tour, of course. It's just that she had to get past the whole Ta-da, you-have-an-unexpected-visitor-from-out-of-town-who-will-be-staying-with-you-for-the-next-little-while-and-possibly-make-your-life-a-misery syndrome.

"Emma?" She narrowed her eyes again. Still clutching to her handbag. Emma really wanted to tell her that she was safe in the her apartment that it was okay to put down the handbag.

But she dared not, of course.

"Yes, Mom," was the best she could do.

"What is going on?"

"Well—"

"Ha! I knew it. Fake. I knew you'd made the whole thing up." She tilted her head up with a smug grin.

"Your dear grandfather kept crying every day about you not getting married, not settling down, not doing anything. Then suddenly. Poof. You have a fiancé. What is it? Money? Inheritance? Was that the deal?"

"What?" Emma's ears burned. But that wasn't the only thing that was fired up. She was heated up to a boiling point inside. She could take no more.

Her eyes widened in shock. "What are you saying? Why would I make up all that stuff? And no, what money are you talking about? There is nothing. It's not about money. What's wrong with you?"

Emma was on the verge of tears. Then she heard bubbling sounds in the bathroom. She clapped her hand on her forehead.

"The bath!"

She sprinted into the bathroom, her mind and emotions still numb with shock. Over her mother. Her fake fiancé. Her tub. She couldn't even do that without a hitch. She'd almost forgotten she was running a bath.

She immediately switched off the faucet. Then she turned to her mother, anger flooding her eyes. Balls of heat seemed to be brewing under her skin. Her legs tingled. Her feet felt numb.

"Mother, why did you come here?"

Just then, the phone started to ring.

"Because, your father left me out of the will. I know he must have left something. Now your grandfather is on his way out. You want me to believe that he's not going to leave you anything? What about that pearl necklace? That was mine and your father stole it from me when we divorced. That thing's worth more than the Hope diamond."

Emma's jaw fell open.

"Well, aren't you gonna answer that? It may just be your fake fiancé."

Emma stood up, too shocked to speak. She walked past her mother to the bedroom and picked up her cordless phone.

Still the words rang in her mind.

Pearl necklace?

Hope Diamond?

This was all too crazy. Too soon.

"Hello?" Emma's head felt sore. Her temples throbbed without mercy.

"Hey, Emma. So sorry I couldn't call you before." She recognised the deep, sexy voice on the other end of the line. God, it was like a fresh wave of hope. After the fiasco she'd just been through, it was as if the Red Sea parted and she was finally able to get through and escape from Pharaoh's mouth—or horses.

"Evan?"

"Evan?" Her mother echoed, listening in to her conversation. Now the look of shock was spread on *her* face.

"Listen, I'm still with my father. There's been...an accident." His voice reflected his extreme exhaustion. He sounded nothing at all like the strong, energetic, confidant boss in New York. It was like he'd just been through hell and back and had to go back to do another round but wasn't quite up for it.

"What? Is he alright?"

"I hope so. I've been at the Dan Baker Center all weekend. Serious crisis. But I'll explain later. Everything go okay with your grandfather? We still on for Friday?"

Emma swallowed. "Um. Yes. Of course. And Gramps is doing fine. Holding on, you know Gramps." Emma tried to play brave.

"Please give your father my love for me. Hope he's feeling better soon." A smile perched on Emma's face, but it was nothing compared to the one in her heart.

Wait a minute. Did he just say the Dan Baker Center? There was only one Dan Baker Center she'd heard about.

The Dan Baker Center for Mental Health. Formerly called The Insane Asylum.

15

Evan sighed and rubbed his forehead when he got off the phone with Emma. He hesitated before going back into the hospital room where his father rested on his bed.

The inpatient mental health unit at the Dan Baker Center for Mental Health was rather serene—not quite what he expected. When he heard his father had been transferred there from the county hospital, he was thinking more along the lines of insane asylum prison décor. Still, he quickly went from royally peeved to royally pleased.

The dim lights, earth-toned tiled floor, the oil paintings of greenery and natural landscapes were surprisingly calming.

Soothing.

Just what he needed on Saturday to settle his nerves by the time he'd arrived to see his father and find out just what happened while he was out of town.

The doctors and nurses were dressed in regular business casual attire. No scrub uniforms like the medical units of regular hospitals.

The whiff of fresh cut flowers caught his nose. The aroma mixed in with the pine scent of disinfectant mingled with the smell of leftover food on trays—mashed potatoes with slices roast beef and gravy with carrots on the side.

He walked closer to the bed, which was elevated to a thirty degree angle. Evan's hands remained shoved in his pants pockets, head tilted, thinking.

Pondering.

What if he hadn't been around at that time to intervene?

Yes, his father was far more subdued, relaxed, restrained than he was that morning when he arrived from New York.

He had planned to give Emma a call when he rose Saturday morning at his condo, but instead he was awakened at four o'clock in the morning by Bianca, his ex, the community mental health nurse he hired to stay overnight to assist his ailing father while he could not be there.

She'd told him that his father started tearing down the drapes in the house and screamed profanities. She rushed to calm him down then went for his anti-neurotic medication used for whenever he had a breakdown or became agitated or in a presumed crisis. Like the one he had.

It was futile.

He'd fought her and knocked her over. Then he went into the kitchen and flung all the pots and pans about.

She was worried he'd hurt himself or do much worse. Bianca called the ER to report his psychiatric crisis. She was lucky—it didn't take as long as she thought it would for the ambulance team to arrive on the scene. They were there in good time and the senior Mr. Fletcher was rushed to the hospital. Later, he was transferred to the Dan Baker Center for a three-day observation.

So far he'd been okay at the facility after the crisis team de-escalated his situation.

Apparently, the doctor said, the problem stemmed form lack of attention. From his son. Yep, attention.

Mr. Fletcher started to behave well when Bianca began to care for him. But then he won her trust over, then started to play tricks with her mind. Just as he'd done with the other psych nurses who visited him.

He could not believe they eventually all fell for the old pretend-to-take-the-pill trick.

Got them every time.

He would pretend to take his pill, then distract them. When they weren't looking he'd either drop it down his shirt, in his pillow, or spit it out, if he did take it.

Discreetly, of course.

He'd even mastered the art of keeping the pill to the side of his mouth. Careful not to dissolve it with his saliva, then he'd discard it as soon as he was in the clear.

The doctor had told Evan that his father simply missed him and felt the recurrence of being abandoned.

All over again.

Only it wasn't abandonment from his ex-wives, he feared. It was abandonment from his own, beloved son.

He figured Evan's moves out to a tee. Evan happened to be around more often and for longer periods of time when his father was having a meltdown or a crisis.

Evan felt a pull at his stomach.

A taste of guilt.

Maybe he had been working too hard with his business. It wasn't as if he were in the beginning stages of his ad agency. Heck, he'd been around for over a decade.

Well established.

Armed with a damn good team at his side.

Why couldn't he be more like Emma? She visited her grandfather, not just once a week or month, but religiously—daily. Often twice a day. It was as if she incorporated it into her daily routine without fail.

Like bathing, eating, working.

"Gramps" was very much a part of her daily life. And she loved him—cherished the time she spent with him. It was as if she'd been given golden nuggets of quality time with her ailing grandfather.

Evan gulped down another lump of guilt. He inched closer to his dad and sat beside him on the bed. He stroked his old man's forehead then leaned over to kiss him on his bold spot.

"Dad, I'm so sorry I wasn't there for you. I'm gonna be around a lot more now. I promise you."

He placed another gentle kiss on his old man's forehead.

The nurse came in and wrote her name on the white board in the room. It was shift change. They worked twelve-hour shifts at that facility. Evan wondered how the medical staff did it. From 7:30 in the morning right up until 7:30 in the evening. That was a long day managing psychiatric crisis and intervention. Working at the office had a bit more flexibility. Yes, he was responsible for client accounts, but not exactly people's lives.

His admiration for the medical and nursing profession ran deep.

The nurse noticed Evan's five o'clock shadow coupled with dark shadows under his eyes. She'd read Mr. Fletcher's chart under the social work notes where it noted Mr. Fletcher's family support system.

"Hi, I'm Calli. You must be Evan."

"Hi, Calli. Nice to meet you," Evan said wearily as he reached over to shake her hand.

He made it a point to be grateful to all the staff who cared for his father. In the past, when his father was an inpatient at a regular hospital's inpatient mental health unit, he'd often bring in treats for the nursing staff.

He even had flowers delivered to thank them for all their meticulous care.

"I'm your father's nurse for the night," she continued and smiled. Her voice was soothing, gentle. "I'm just on rounds to see how the patients are doing. I see your father's still sound asleep." The nurse's expression turned to one of concern when she glanced at Evan's face.

"You okay?"

"Oh, I'm good," he said in a voice so low, it was barely audible. He still held his father's hand and stroked his dad's arm as he lay still, sedated.

"You know—you should probably try to get some rest. You've been here all weekend, I understand."

"I'm good, really. I need to spend a little time with my old man, that's all."

"Have you been home at all over the weekend? Even for a break?" She looked aghast. Concerned dressed her face. "Is there anyone else who could stand in for you and give you a respite?"

Evan thought of Emma. A strange thing to do at that time.

At times like this it would be so nice to have a caring companion by his side. A good-hearted person who had the patience and unselfish, noble heart to stick around when things got rough.

Someone to support you. To comfort you.

He didn't know why but she just popped into his mind. Then there was that whole wedding bit he'd committed to for this week. He mentally clapped his hand on his forehead.

He shivered to think of getting married—even if it were for pretence. Just look at what getting married did to his old man.

Talk about bad timing.

Still, it wasn't as if it was going to be a real wedding.

"No. There's no one else," he answered the nurse quietly. A trace of humility laced his voice.

Evan was then slammed with another horrible thought. If he wasn't around at all.

Out of the picture.

Non-existent.

Who would watch out for his old man? Who would be there for him? With him in his time of emotional turmoil? Who would lovingly put up with his verbal abuse—something he simply couldn't help because it was a part of his symptoms. His illness.

Who would give him unconditional love? Gentle care.

Unadulterated compassion.

He'd been wrapped up and absorbed in his business affairs for so long. But the truth was, work couldn't provide comfort at night or a substitute caregiver for his old man, could it?

Work was magnificent.

Fulfilling.

It was something incredible to do. Something to become. A challenge. A provider for his financial and egotistical needs. But even after all of this—clearly work wasn't everything.

In Evan's book, if you can't care for your own family, then whatever success you do have outside the home was virtually meaningless.

Pointless.

Evan spent the next fifteen minutes speaking with the nurse about his father's plan of care. He ordered dinner again for the patriarch of his dwindling family. His dad's favorite was Mexican. Old Mr. Fletcher wasn't very fond of the hospital food—not that Evan could blame him.

Evan hadn't checked his BlackBerry all weekend. He'd wanted to focus all his energy on supporting his dad through the meltdown, his crisis. He'd already e-mailed Lucinda, the receptionist and office manager, as to when he would return to the office. As well as where he could be paged in dire emergency.

That was sufficient enough, in his book.

16

Evan would be back in the office on Tuesday—tomorrow. But then there was that little fake wedding thing he'd promised Emma. He estimated it would probably take no more than an hour, tops, if that.

Still, he had to hand it to Emma. She had guts and was all heart. To do what she was about to do. Just to make her grandfather happy. What a woman! She'd make some lucky guy happy one day. Too bad he wasn't the marrying-type.

Right now work would just have to be on hold for a little while. Evan already had a good team working on his accounts. They were independent enough that he didn't have to babysit them or hold their hands through client negotiations.

He just couldn't let his old man down. Not now.

Besides, if it weren't for his father, where would he be now?

His father practically raised him on his own. He never got a chance to know his real mother. She passed when he was born. And those substitutes who came by over the years?

The now ex-Mrs. Fletchers.

In Evan's eyes, that was all a joke. They each seemed to have their own agenda and being the dutiful wife and doting mother to a child who was not their own, that didn't seem to fit into their world. The hubby and kid combo wasn't on their menu.

He tried to quell the thoughts for the sake of anger management. He felt heat rise in his chest with each recollection of his former stepmothers.

Not good.

When his father woke—Evan didn't want to be caught with a disgruntled look spread on his face. He certainly didn't want to convey a spirit of contempt. He smoothed out his expression and tried to grasp at a more pleasant thought in his head.

Emma.

New York.

They were the most memorable nights of passion he'd ever had. And he'd had many in his lifetime thus far. There was something special about her. He couldn't quite pinpoint it. She would be the one to drive him to the mad house if he allowed himself to deepen his feelings for her.

Evan rubbed his forehead as he sat watching his father. He was seated in the chair, the room was dim, soothing. Calm. He felt like he would need a rest, too. Not just from the exhaustion of the weekend, but his recurring thoughts.

Why couldn't he banish Emma Wiggins from his mind?

"So, that was your fiancé!?" Ms. Wiggins cast her daughter a disbelieving look. "You really are getting married?"

"Well, of course, I am. Why would I lie?" Emma stopped herself cold. She swallowed hard but the lump in her throat remained—with a vengeance.

Guilt 101.

Of course, the truth was, she was lying like a rug in the middle of a Persian rug gallery.

Ms. Wiggins scanned Emma's cosy but small apartment. "I thought you were- Listen, I'm sorry I jumped to conclusions. You hadn't mentioned anything to me about having a fiancé and getting married. I heard about if through your grandfather."

She laughed nervously. "I thought your grandfather cooked this whole thing up to avoid giving me back the pearl necklace your grandmother got married in. You know. She handed it to me but somehow your father got a hold of it when we broke up and returned it to your grandmother. Now, I'm told that you have it, for your wedding day."

Ms. Wiggins plopped herself down on Emma's cream-colored couch with the oversized cushions. She had to push one of the cushions aside so that she could squeeze her bottom on the chair comfortably.

There, Ms. Wiggins faced a twenty inch flat screen TV, a small glass coffee table with a few pictures of Emma's grandparents on their wedding day, Emma's parents on their wedding day, and a snapshot of happier times.

Her parents when they were together.

A close-knit family unit.

Before the messy divorce. A picture of Emma at three-years-old with her puppy, Ruffles, before he passed away. She missed that dog.

Ms. Wiggins reached over to grasp the picture of her own wedding day. Water misted her eyes. Sadness glazed her expression. She was suddenly aware that her daughter's eyes were on her and promptly shifted her expression.

"Aw. Well, isn't that sweet," she sighed. "A picture of happier times." She almost voiced it nonchalantly.

Her mother was ever so good at hiding her true emotions. Emma could never understand why she wanted to though. She wondered if it had something to do with her crippling paranoia.

Empathy settled itself in Emma's heart. "Yes, it was happier times, wasn't it, Mom?" She felt sorry for the loss of her own father. So young. She hardly remembered him.

Her mother seemed unhearing of Emma's comment and continued to scan the pictures throughout the living area of the apartment. A photo of a vacation spot with her friends, including Genie, hung over by the wall.

Ms. Wiggins looked aghast. "Where is Evan?"

"What? I told you, Mom, he's not here." Emma just remembered the call. "He's at the hospital with his father. Been there all weekend." Well, at least that was the full truth. No lies in that bologna sandwich.

The truth was, Evan had been really preoccupied with tending to a sick relative in the middle of a health crisis. Who could blame him for keeping away and focusing on his loved one?

Emma certainly understood to a tee, the complexity of caregiving for an ailing family member.

"No. No." Ms. Wiggins shook her head. She got up again and moved over to the old, crooked bookshelf— one that Emma assembled herself.

Something Emma swore she would never do again since she always found herself unlucky to get a box with missing screws or screws and parts that didn't quite mesh together as displayed on the cover of the box. She vowed to pay extra for ready-assembled products in the future since DIY was not her strong suit.

Ms. Wiggins eyed some more pictures displayed face out in front of some books. Ms. Wiggins noticed that Emma had a lot of mismatched furniture in her apartment. It was neat. Just humble.

"Where are the pictures of you and your fiancé?"

Oops!

Emma gulped.

She hadn't figured she would have anyone visit out of the blue and certainly didn't think she would have to answer such questions.

She knew her grandfather would be too ill to get a pass to leave the hospital to visit her. She hadn't factored any of that in.

Then, a flash struck her.

New York.

Emma leaped to her feet. Excitement rose in her chest. She had her digital camera with the images of her trip to New York—with Evan.

Emma and Evan, having a blast in the Big Apple. As a couple—well, sort of.

She scrambled over to her bag that was plopped over by the dining room chair to locate the silver Panasonic camera—the one she'd purchased when she graduated college after being one of the last people on earth to use the old-fashioned 35mm.

She powered on her camera when she finally had it in her grasp. Her heart racing, her feet twitching. Her eyes narrowing. Waiting. Anticipating. Longing to prove her point. Provide the proof.

The lying proof.

Nothing.

No image appeared on the camera's display screen.

Her heart leaped. Then plunged.

Her mother drew closer.

"Something wrong, dear?"

"Oh. Um. No. Nothing's wrong." She frowned. She fidgeted with the buttons on the camera.

Still nothing.

Where were those images? *Just my luck. That's what happens, I suppose, when you concoct a soup of lies. You get to chug down a bitter remedy of karma.*

She was about to tell her mother the whole, unadulterated truth when the images appeared on the screen.

Like a miracle.

"Oh, he's handsome." Her mother leaned in closer to get a look. "He's drop-dead gorgeous!"

Her mother clasped her hands to her chest.

"Congratulations!" Her mother threw her a huge bear hug. The first, Emma noticed, since her arrival.

Emma stopped cold.

What had she just done?

Mentally, she clapped her hand over her forehead. Oh, great. I've just dug myself in deeper to this hole of deceit. How am I ever going to climb out of it?

She swallowed hard, a thick lump of guilt and felt the bitterness ride down her throat.

Oh, how she wished she were getting married to Evan—for real.

17

Evan leaned back in his swivel chair in the boardroom, his team encircling him around the table. He eyed Emma.

She looked ravishing—but she was a pleasant distraction he didn't need right now. He had missed a couple of days at the office on business and had to get back on top of things.

He had a lot on his mind. His father's downward spiral—which thankfully had tapered off. Doctor's reported he was currently stable. Then there was that fake wedding. Painful as it was, he'd go along with it.

It was Tuesday morning and the Texas sun blazed through the tall office glass windows of the boardroom exposing the beautiful township of Mercy Springs.

Evan noticed it highlighted Emma's best features. Her lustrous, ebony curls glistened. Her hair looked so healthy, so vibrant. Much like her.

The team discussed action plans and brainstormed ideas for upcoming product launches for various clients. Each member present talked about what specific project he or she was engaged in and for which client.

Lucinda bolted through the glass double door of the boardroom. "Sorry, Evan. You have a call on line one from Leanne Daniels."

"Leanne Daniels?" Evan was puzzled. He didn't recognize the name. He couldn't place it from his roster of friends, family, colleagues, casual acquaintances. And often those were some of the finer details he seldom forgot. Very little slipped his sharp mind.

"Did she say where she's calling from or what it's about?"

"Well, no. She just said it was a personal matter." Lucinda waited for a response. Her earphone piece still dangling from her ear.

Evan noticed Lucinda often would leave reception to personally deliver certain phone call messages though he didn't quite understand her rationale for it. Still, he didn't feel too easy about leaving the reception area open. Especially if a client walked in or a courier had an urgent package to deliver or ship out.

He was tempted to tell her to take a message that he was in a meeting. But something, he wasn't quite sure what it was, but something compelled him to take the call.

Emma froze as she sat glued to her chair in the boardroom, her eyes widened as she ignored her notes in front of her. She was about to deliver her ideas for projects she was working on when Lucinda walked in.

But it wasn't that. She felt a lump climb in her throat. A knot tied itself in the pit of her belly, squeezing her last bit of nerve.

Leanne Daniels. Leanne Daniels.
Where on earth have I heard that name before?

It wasn't an ex-girlfriend of his. She didn't think it was. But she knew that name from somewhere. And it bugged her that it was on the tip of her tongue but buried at the back of her mind—it wouldn't depart her lips.

She knew she heard it before. But why did it cause the hairs to stiffen up on her due-for-a-wax legs?

Evan excused himself to take the call in his office. "Okay, take five everyone. Let's get back to discuss the week's projects."

Emma excused herself to make a quick trip to the restroom. She'd whipped by her office afterwards to make a quick phone call to the florist. She had ordered flowers for the occasion on Friday. Her wedding day. Her grandfather's proud moment in his last days.

She knew how much her grandfather cherished his gardening and flowers. She ordered the variety he'd be proud of.

She even went as far as to get his old favourite pin-striped suit altered. He'd lost so much weight since the long battle with his illness, but he always talked about that striped suit. The one he bought when he came to America and worked hard during the early days. The one he took her grandmother out on a special date in.

Ever since she could remember, he'd told her that he would walk her down the aisle in that suit. He had it dry-cleaned and would take it out of his closet when he was much stronger and admire it. There was just something about that suit. For some reason, it meant a whole lot to him.

Which in turn meant a lot to Emma.

Now, in his final days, he'd be able to wear it the way he wanted. Only thing she hoped she wouldn't go straight to hell for not being up front and honest about not really marrying Evan or not actually being engaged.

Tears from her large, soft brown eyes spilled down her cheeks. She dried them quickly.

How could she not be moved? Touched? Affected by all of this? She so wanted this to work—for his sake.

This was Gramps' dying wish. The man who sacrificed everything for her. To make her life as normal and happy as could be. Especially when her own parents deserted her.

And yes, she'd secretly wished she were marrying Evan for real. She had feelings for him she could not explain. She'd always had them and fantasizing about a way to make him real to her in a relationship.

That was why it seemed to roll off her tongue so easy when her grandfather asked who she would be marrying. In her mind, they had a relationship. In reality, they worked closely with each other. And they respected and looked out for each other. It didn't seemed that farfetched.

As Emma hung up the phone in her office to get ready to head back into the meeting, a shocking thought paralyzed her.

She knew where she'd heard the name Leanne Daniels!

Emma winced. She felt faint.

It was the hospital's chaplain. The very person who would be performing her ceremony. Evan still didn't know exactly what he would be getting into—yet.

.

18

Emma's heart thumped heard when she heard the heavy footsteps stomping towards her office.

It was Evan.

Anger dressed his face. His hands shoved in his pockets. He looked like he was ready to explode. Emma hadn't seen this side of him before. His eyes glistened wild like a boar's. Horror crept up her. She didn't think he'd respond quite like this, but then again.... Another thought slapped her hard in the head.

He was gamophobic.

She was forcing him to marry her.

Evan slammed the door shut and closed the blinds of Emma's office. He didn't know how he was going to contain himself.

"You mind telling me what's going on?"

The blood vessel in his forehead was about to explode—if that was at all possible. Oh, he felt it, alright.

"Evan. I…I'm so sorry. I tried to tell you but…"

"Tell me what? You were forcing me to marry you?"

Emma felt shattered inside. She could not think.

"Please give me a chance to explain, Evan."

"I don't think I can listen to any more of your lies, Emma. You tricked me. The chaplain at the hospital started asking me all these questions. Wanting ID and everything. Date of birth. I thought you were just going to pretend we were married or getting married."

He paced with his hands shoved in his pockets, frantic. Occasionally pulling them out of his pockets to thrash them about the air. "I didn't know you were really going to go through with it."

"I'm so sorry, Evan. I should have told you everything but—"

"But nothing. You tricked me." He was so angry he didn't know if he could think straight or listen to her. He should have taken time out to deep breathe or something, but oh, this was deeper than words. This stuff kicked him hard where it hurt the most.

He narrowed his eyes in disgust and pointed a finger at her. "You're just like all the rest. Lies. Deceit. I'm not gonna be part of your little game, Emma. Guess you'll be walking down the aisle alone on Friday."

He stormed out as hard as he blew in.

Emma collapsed in her chair.

Shock.

She could not move, speak, or think.

She was shaken to the core. She'd just lost one of the most valuable relationships she'd ever had.

And what about Gramps? Now he'd never forgive her. He'll go to the grave angry. Sad. Oh, God, will he die of a broken heart? She'd heard of these things happening. She clasped her hands to her chest. She had to perish the thought.

Did she deserve it?

That's what happened when you told huge lies—
even if it was to help someone. So you think. She realized
she may have made things worse. How could she face
Gramps? Or Evan? Did that mean that she was fired?

And how could she ever face herself again?

Okay, he does have a phobia about marriage. And
what did she do? Try to force him to marry her. For real.

Oh, God!

Later, Evan left the office early and drove up to see his
old man who was now out of the hospital and back home.
He needed someone to talk to about his own personal
crisis.

He felt like he was about to explode.

He turned off the ignition and grabbed his
BlackBerry then flung it on the passenger seat. He didn't
feel like talking to anyone. Except his old man. He
slammed the car door shut and walked up to the stone
driveway leading to his father's home. He sucked in a deep
breath.

Did he have the guts to follow through with what
he was about to do?

19

Three days later, the flowers in the visitor lounge looked beautiful with the colorful decorations. A mini wedding banquet room.

It was Friday, the day of the ceremony that never would happen. Emma sucked in a deep breath as she walked up the death pathway, so she'd thought, to deliver the terrible news to her grandfather.

Prepared for the worst.

The last few days were a blur. She hadn't heard from Evan. He hadn't returned any of her calls. And her mother said she would be staying with a friend until the wedding. Someone she hadn't seen in a while. Genie was studying for finals. She'd felt so alone during the most difficult crisis she'd have to face.

Alone.

She would have to tell her Gramps that she lied to him about the whole damn thing. The more she walked up and saw the smiles of the nurses and patients congratulating her about the ceremony that would happen in the afternoon, the more her stomach churned in agony.

She could not do this.

She hesitated when Mr. H approached her and told her he was looking forward to seeing her and Evan get married in the hospital visitor lounge. Her grandfather's room would be too small. He told her that he and her grandfather were excited and trying on ties for the special occasion. Of course, the nurse had to help Emma's grandfather.

The aroma of the fresh cut flowers, the whiff of the hospital pine smell, it was all calming. But she needed a whole lot more for her nerves. The balloons and laid out table looked so lovely. Weddings R Us couldn't have done it better. Wait a minute, she thought. The placemats looked like something from her client but she couldn't have been sure. She did a double-take and blinked it off.

She walked up to the door. Tears flooded her eyes.

"Baby, what's wrong with my little pumpkin? You should be getting ready for this afternoon."

"Oh, Gramps. I'm so sorry." She was about to spill everything.

"You know, it's only good luck to cry on your wedding day when you are getting married. Not before." A deep, low voice sounded from behind her.

It was Evan.

He was there! Dressed in a fine evening suit. Black tie affair. As if he were the... groom? He looked dashing, hands shoved in his pocket. His dimpled smile, gorgeous black hair slicked back, leaning casually against the countertop behind the door. He had been talking to her grandfather apparently.

"What? What's going on?" Emma looked puzzled.

"Oh, pumpkin, I had the most amazing talk with your fiancé here."

Evan didn't take his eyes off Emma. She swallowed. She didn't dare spoil anything.

"You know sometimes people do foolish things, but when it's for a good reason, a good cause, sometimes you just gotta know when to let things slide. Especially if she means a lot to you."

Just then, Genie walked in with a garment bag holding her bridal attire. "Well, Cinderella, you just gonna stand there? We have a wedding to attend."

Emma turned to Evan and mouthed the words thank you and I'm so sorry I put you through this.

He whispered to her as he held her and told her it was alright. A little later he pulled her aside.

"You were right," he said, "I was hiding behind fear. I had a long chat with my old man the other night. He kinda put things into perspective. You're not like other girls. I was upset about being burned one too many times."

"Oh, Evan! I was wrong to not be upfront about everything in the first place. I shoved my foot in my mouth and got you into this."

"No. No. Well, yeah, you did. But they way I see it, you did it because your heart's in the right place. Your ideas are a little off but..." he teased her.

She brushed his arm playfully.

"I wanna do this for real." His voice was deep and throaty and sent tingly shivers zipping about her midsection. He turned to face her, his dark, sexy eyes holding her gaze intently. "I love you, Emma. And...crazy as it may sound right now, given the circumstances that we're here today, I do wanna be with you for as long as time can handle. I can't keep living my life afraid because of things not working out or because of the past. And I can't live my life through the men in my family who've dealt with the curse. I'll explain later," he told her when he noticed the puzzled look on her face.

She smiled.

"So do I. I love you, too, Evan. Really, I do. I think I have since I first saw you."

He gave her an appreciative smile. "Just promise me one thing."

"Anything."

"The next time you plan on making drastic changes to my personal life, do you mind letting me in on what you're doing?"

She smiled and reached up to hug his neck.

"I promise."

Shadonna Richards

Bestselling author Shadonna Richards has a B.A. degree in Psychology and a diploma in Nursing. She enjoys reading and writing about the magic of romance and the power of love. She is the author of the non-fiction books, *A Gift of Hope* and *Think & Be Happy: 365 Empowering Thoughts to Lift Your Spirit* (an Amazon Kindle #1 Bestseller in Meditation). Winner of Harlequin's *So You Think You Can Write 2010 Day Two Challenge*, she is a member of the Romance Writers of America. *An Unexpected Bride* became a Top 5 Kindle bestseller in Romance and is her first novel. It has sold over 25,000 copies in its first five months on Kindle. She's a proud mommy and wife and lives in Canada with her husband and son. You can visit her at www.shadonnarichards.blogspot.com and join her mailing list for updates, giveaways and news on upcoming releases.

SHADONNA RICHARDS

13659982R00104

Made in the USA
Lexington, KY
14 February 2012